DON'T FALL FOR THE DOCTOR

A SWEET, CLEAN ROMANCE

LACEY BOLT

SECOND TURN PUBLISHING, LLC

TO LEARN MORE

To learn more about new releases and Lacey's goings on, sign up for her newsletter at http://www. laceybolt.com/doctor_signup.

CHAPTER 1

"Ashley, you're twenty minutes late."

Ashley inhaled slowly while raising her coffee cup to her lips. If Gwen, her supervisor, felt entitled to start her commentary before Ashley even clocked in for work, she would enjoy her coffee while listening. The bitter drink didn't have the usual splash of milk, but she'd had enough nutmeg and cinnamon in her spice drawer to add a little extra flavor before she came into work.

"My shift doesn't start for another ten minutes. I'm early." The clock on the wall confirmed the time.

If she were late, she'd accept the consequences. But she never arrived late, even though every ounce of her body dreaded coming to this thankless job every day.

The housekeeping phone rang, the sound echoing off the metal lockers near Gwen. Ashley started to sidestep Gwen to open her locker, but Gwen blocked her.

"No, you are late. I switched the schedule last night. You aren't on the inpatient wing today. I switched you to clean the cardiac clinic. You needed to be here twenty minutes ago."

Ashley tried to hide her frown by taking another sip of coffee. It really needed milk—creamer would have been better, but cost too much.

If only she hadn't used up all her milk last night when she tried that new crepe recipe.

Gwen stared at Ashley, lips pursed and nostrils flaring.

"Can you switch me back to the inpatient clinic?" She held her breath. Any unit in the hospital was better than the cardiac clinic.

Gwen scowled. "If you think you can do a better job managing the housekeeping unit of this hospital, then go ahead and talk to the administration."

Ashley opened her mouth, then closed it quickly. She'd only give Gwen an excuse to cut her hours if she argued anymore. "Fine. Cardiac clinic? I'll head right over."

"If you can't be here on time, then I can't count on you anymore. I'll give your shift to someone else. Someone who is ready to work when they get here." Gwen gestured at Ashley's coffee.

"I'm ready. I'll be on time tomorrow." Ashley reached past Gwen to her locker and hastily placed her coffee mug and purse inside.

Gwen continued to stare at Ashley. Ashley's stomach sank as she realized what Gwen wanted.

She gritted her teeth but parted her lips to say, "I'm sorry for being late. It won't happen again." Ashley's face burned as she spat out the words.

Gwen grunted and walked away. Ashley waited until the locker room door shut behind Gwen, then sat on the bench and allowed herself a few last sips of coffee. The last dredges were barely warm, but every last ounce of caffeine would help today.

She would definitely have to buy milk on the way home

from work. Not a large one, just a small container to get through the next week until payday.

On second thought, maybe she should get used to drinking coffee without milk. If she did get accepted to graduate school for social work, she would have to cut down on expenses even more than she already did. She had enough saved in her bank account, with the help of massive student loans, if she could manage to tighten her belt even more.

Gwen's voice floated through the door of the locker room. Ashley jumped and slammed her locker door shut. She still needed all the work hours Gwen would allow her, and that meant staying on Gwen's good side.

Ashley slipped out the back exit of the locker room, feet heavy and muscles already aching from the thought of spending the day in the cardiac clinic.

CHAPTER 2

"Explain yourself." The chief cardiologist's stern voice removed the last hint of a smile from Dr. Michael Tobers' face.

Dr. Evans, the chief cardiologist, threw a magazine on top of the large mahogany desk. Michael stared at his own image on the open pages. A lump formed in his throat, but he forced himself to lean back in the chair and stretch out his legs.

He did nothing wrong. He covered all his bases before the article came out. Sure, he forgot to check with HR until after it was too late to stop the article. But thanks to that meeting last week, he knew he was in the clear.

The vein popping out of Dr. Evans's forehead suggested otherwise. One of the nurses warned him about Dr. Evans's temper months ago, during his first shift at the hospital. He hadn't believed the rumors about his rigid adherence to any and all rules until now.

"I checked with HR first, and they said there was nothing in my contract prohibiting this." He crossed and then uncrossed his arms before forcing a laugh through his lips.

"They could have picked a better tagline, but . . ." He shrugged, letting the words fade away. He maintained steady eye contact, refusing to let the chief see that his intimidating tactics were working.

Michael's ears started to ring, a warning of what was to come. He scratched his ear, but the noise continued. The tightness in his chest was building. His heart began to beat faster than it had during his three-mile run that morning, and now the walls in the room felt suffocatingly close.

"Anything else? I have patients to see. Oh, and I noticed that no one cleaned up the vomit in the exam room from my first patient." His voice took on a higher pitch than usual. He fought the urge to get up and run out of the office. If the chief didn't back down soon, annoying him would be the least of Michael's problems.

A few seconds passed as the chief glared at Michael. Finally, the chief broke eye contact and let his hands fall to his side. Dr. Evans turned around to face the large windows of his office and spoke, but the words were too hard to understand over the ringing in his ears and the sound of his heartbeat.

Michael cleared his throat and stood up, cutting Dr. Evans off. "Mind if I take this with me?" He grabbed the magazine where it still lay on the large desk and walked out the door, ignoring the sounds still coming from the chief.

The closest stairway was down the hall and through the door on the left. Michael ignored the people in the hall. He ran around them until he reached the heavy door of the stairwell and raced down several steps to a landing, far away from the cardiology clinic.

The cement floor was cold as he sat. What else had the therapist said? *Focus on something solid to touch, and count breaths slowly. Breathe in slowly, breathe out slowly. This will pass.*

He placed all his attention on his breath.

There was no air in the stairway. No oxygen was going into his lungs. Focusing on his breath was pointless. His chest was too tight, and if something didn't happen soon, he would pass out.

His vision clouded, and he could barely see his hands in front of his face. Was this really a panic attack or something more? This was unbelievable. After all those years of medical training, he should know the difference between a heart attack and a panic attack. But his chest hurt so badly.

He moved his hand from his chest to the cold concrete floor and focused on breathing through his nose. Slow and steady . . . in and out . . .

Finally, Michael's vision started to clear, and the muted noises from the hospital began to reach his ears. A door slammed a few floors above, and two people spoke on the stairwell in quiet voices. A second door slam was followed by silence as the owners of the voices left the stairway.

Michael pulled his phone from his pocket. That was too close. Nothing like this had happened in months, not since he had lost a patient in the operating room.

Gary.

The case had been complicated, and he knew the odds were against him, but Gary's wife said Michael was their last hope. Their last chance for a long life together. They knew the chances of surviving the surgery were slim, but they still wanted the procedure.

Michael had done the same procedure earlier that year for a patient who was in worse health. That patient survived and was now thriving. The medical association gave him an award for his success with that case, and he wrote two separate academic articles about the procedure.

But Gary hadn't survived. Michael spent a week coping

with one anxiety attack after another last year until his therapist helped him get things under control again.

A little run-in with his boss shouldn't be enough to upset him. Not like this.

No one died. No one suffered.

His boss was just mad that he was featured in a local magazine that people probably didn't even read.

Whatever his boss thought, his record spoke for itself. He was an unstoppable cardiologist—one of the best in the region. People traveled hours to see him. They came to him when other cardiologists gave up hope.

Would the patients still trust him if they knew that he had anxiety attacks?

I am one of the best. Michael repeated the words with each measured inhale. If only he actually believed that.

Michael pulled out his cell phone, wiped the sweat off his hands, and selected a name from his contacts.

"Bill, call me back. I almost got chewed out by hospital administration; they aren't happy about that article. Never should have done it. But you talked me into it, and you need to help me out of this mess. Call me when you are out of surgery."

CHAPTER 3

Ashley opened the back door to the notoriously demanding cardiology clinic, channeling her inner spy. When she was a kid, she would sneak into her parents' bedroom to snoop. Now, she used those childhood skills to sneak into the cardiology unit. If all went well, no one would notice her. Particularly Dr. Evans.

The clinic hallway was empty. She let out a quiet breath and tilted her head. Soft chatter floated in her direction, most likely from the nursing staff's morning meeting in the conference room. They'd come spilling out to the hallway at any moment.

She crept towards the noise, heart pounding in her throat. She stopped when she reached the cleaning supply closet and then slowly opened the door, which let out a loud squeak. She froze. The quiet chatter from the conference room continued. Wiping her forehead, she opened the door the rest of the way, and proceeded to toss a few random boxes on her cart. If all went well, anyone who saw her would assume that she'd already been working for the past half hour.

She glanced at the list attached to the wall, then grabbed an empty bucket, placed it under the faucet, and turned on the water. She leaned against her cleaning cart and closed her eyes. The slow stream of water gurgled like a waterfall on a sandy, warm beach. Did Dr. Evans know how to swim? Or any of the other cardiologists? Probably. But if they were all stuck on a deserted, tropical island, she would definitely push them into the water to find out. And if they were stuck on that island together, they'd all soon come begging her for help. No one else could take a scattering of fruits, vegetables, and fish and turn them into a gourmet meal. They'd be forced to talk to her like an actual human instead of ignoring her.

"Ashley!"

Ashley bolted upright and stumbled. She reached for the cart to catch herself but pulled too hard. The cart fell over, knocking the half-filled bucket onto its side. A cold sensation washed over her feet as the water spread.

Ashley muttered under her breath and turned off the faucet. She faced her friend and tried her best to look stern. "Kelly, you surprised me. Are you on clinic duty with me today?"

Kelly shook her finger at Ashley in a motherly manner. "Wipe that look off your face. It's only water."

"It's only water to you because you aren't the one who's about to get fired." Ashley grabbed the cart and pushed it upright. She bent down to examine the wheel. The bracket attaching the wheel to the cart was even more bent than it had been yesterday.

"It's just the two of us today. Jean called in sick." Kelly glanced around and lowered her voice. "I covered for you earlier, so no one knows that you're late. Everything ok?"

"Everything's fine. Gwen just changed the schedule and

never bothered to tell me." Ashley started picking up the fallen items and piled them on the cart.

"Well, don't worry about a thing. I told Dr. Evans that you were running to the main supply closet to restock on a few of the cleaning supplies."

"Thanks. I owe you."

"I'll take payment in the form of brownies." Kelly grinned. "Hand me the mop. I'll get the water over here. Any news about graduate school?"

"Haven't heard a thing yet. Thought I'd at least hear something by now. A rejection is better than just not knowing."

"Don't talk like that. Of course you'll get in. I believe in you, and Emily does too. She wouldn't have recommended you to her former social work school if she didn't think you'd get in."

Ashley shrugged. What was there to say? Either she'd get accepted into a social work graduate school or spend her days cleaning and trying to figure out what would make her happy.

Kelly leaned in close again. "Cover for me? I missed breakfast and am starving. I need to run to the cafeteria, shouldn't take more than five minutes."

"Of course. But I put some of my homemade breakfast bars in the staff fridge. They're better than anything you'll find in the cafeteria." Her grandma's recipe never failed to impress.

"Ashley, you are a lifesaver."

"Ok, go, I got this." Ashley pulled the mop out of Kelly's hand.

First, clean up the watery mess in the hallway. Watery messes meant an increased risk of someone falling, getting hurt, suing the hospital, and losing her job. The vomit in the exam room would need to wait.

Mop up excess water. Check. Empty dirty water down the drain. Check. Fill the bucket with clean water and sanitizing soap. Check. Shoot, forgot to put up the wet floor signs. Ok, that's done now. Check. What next? That's right, mop the floor to clean and sanitize the area . . .

"What are you doing?" A large shadow appeared over the wet floor.

Ashley's heart skipped a beat as she faced the man. His red face was lined with a bead of sweat. Dr. Evans.

"Give me one good reason why you are mopping the hallway floor and not cleaning the exam rooms? Room one needs cleaning before the next patient is seen, and Dr. Tobers just told me that room four has vomit! It's been there for seven minutes. What's the hold-up? Go!" Dr. Evans yelled loud enough for patients in the waiting room to hear, not to mention everyone in the staff meeting down the hall.

Words caught in Ashley's mouth, and her legs froze. Dr. Evans grabbed Ashley's supply cart and pushed down the hallway to exam room four, placing it in front of the open door. He turned back to her, arms crossed against his chest and face bright red.

Ashley bit her lip and followed. One of the nurses shouted something down the hall to Dr. Evans, and another nurse stuck his head into the hall from one of the exam rooms. She made brief eye contact with Dr. Tobers, the cardiologist who thought every woman in the hospital wanted to date him just because he looked like an underwear model. He stood at the far end of the hallway, his nose wrinkled like he could actually smell the vomit from his location.

She looked down at her feet and kept trudging down the hall. Being reprimanded at work was one thing. Being humiliated and spoken to as if she was a child in front of an audience was another.

If Dr. Evans were caught on the deserted island with her,

she'd burn his portion of fish and tropical fruit. Then drop the food in the sand.

Who was she kidding? She'd never burn food on purpose.

CHAPTER 4

Michael stood alone at the end of the hallway and watched the scene unfold between Dr. Evans and Ashley. If he had any backbone at all, he'd march up to Dr. Evans and demand that he treated Ashley with respect.

After that, he'd turn to Ashley and finally ask her out. He could find a way to make it work. He could balance the overwhelming demands of the hospital and a personal life.

But no, there couldn't be balance. He made the choice years ago to devote his life to his patients. He took the Hippocratic Oath to do no harm and always care for his patients. Women were a liability—a distraction.

He had enough to deal with. His entire body protested as he turned and walked to the empty provider room, which was equipped with a few small desks set up with computers for charting in-between patients. His next patient wasn't due for another ten minutes, which wasn't nearly enough time to recover from the anxiety attack. But he didn't want to risk Dr. Evans's wrath again by canceling his appointments today and going home on sick leave.

He pulled up the first patient's chart on the computer when a movement by the door caught his eye. He didn't have to look up to know who was there; the scent of cheap perfume and the annoying tap of fingernails on the open exam room door revealed all the information he needed to know. Theresa was back from vacation.

"Well, today must be your lucky day. I'm assigned to assist you with your patients this morning. Now you won't have to deal with any of the other nurses. Just me." She sat down confidently on one of the vacant chairs next to his work-station.

Michael managed to silence the growl that formed in his throat. Instead, he stared at the screen. She continued talking anyway.

"You would not believe everything that happened on my vacation. The beach was amazing, and the weather was absolutely perfect. I even got to work on my tan every day. See how tan I look?" She pulled up her sleeve to reveal her wrist and forearm.

His eyes automatically moved to her arm, and she smiled smugly, leaning in farther. His stomach churned. He turned back to the computer and started typing.

"I'm tan all over. Well, almost all over, if you know what I mean." She let out a small giggle that sounded like nails running across a chalkboard.

Michael didn't even try to hold back the groan this time as he rolled his eyes. The last thing he wanted to do was think about her in a swimsuit.

"Shouldn't you be in the nurses' morning meeting?"

She shrugged and settled back in the chair. "Those meetings are always so boring. I figured I'd skip it and chat with you. I wanted to make sure I'm available to help you this morning."

"Feel free to go back to the meeting. I'm trying to review a few charts before my next patient." Hopefully, she would get the hint and leave.

"Of course you are." She crossed her legs and started examining her manicured nails. "Always so serious and full of business. You should really relax more. A few of us are getting together after work Friday. You should come out and join us."

"I'm busy Friday. I need to finish reviewing this chart now."

"Don't worry. You have plenty of time to review that chart. I can't bring your next patient into the exam room until the mess is all cleaned up. You should have seen Dr. Evans a few minutes ago! He was so mad. That girl is cleaning our clinic today, and she already made a huge mess. She's so clumsy. I'm surprised she hasn't been fired already." Her annoying giggle echoed in his ears again.

Michael gritted his teeth. He needed to tread carefully. He witnessed Theresa relentlessly attack another nurse last month when both women were interested in the medical supply representative. Apparently, Shelia started to flirt with the guy even though she knew that Theresa liked him. Or at least that's what he, and the rest of the clinic, heard during one of many loud arguments in the break room.

In the days that followed, Michael could barely walk around the clinic without finding Shelia crying. It was painfully awkward to walk into an exam room, which he thought was empty, and find an adult woman crying in the corner.

Shelia transferred to another section of the hospital one week later. Unfortunately, Theresa switched her gaze to Michael. He knew very little about women, but he did know that Theresa's interest in him was likely to disappear as quickly as it started. And until she found a new target, any woman who might stand between Theresa and her happily-ever-after dream would have a target on her back.

He would not let Ashley succumb to the same fate as Sheila. "I'm more interested in getting my work done than hearing about drama."

"Hmph." Theresa pouted and crossed her arms. "Don't be mad at me for laughing at her. I know you used to like her. I don't know why. She's a hot mess. You could do so much better."

A sour taste took over his mouth. He narrowed his eyes and frowned at her. He needed to do this right. Swallowing first, he chose his words carefully. "I have no interest in engaging in workplace relationships."

She smirked and leaned forward, her eyes unblinking. "Me neither. But there's no need for anyone at work to know our personal business. Some things are better kept secret."

Michael hit the button on the computer to log off and stood abruptly. "I'm going to check the exam room and get to work. I suggest you do the same."

He walked to the door with her close on his heels. The day was already wearing on him. First the panic attack, and now Theresa.

At least Ashley was in the clinic today. Even though he would never have the time for a relationship, her presence still made him feel hopeful. Like he could have everything. A career he loved, a woman he loved even more, possibly even kids one day.

But he knew better. Besides, a woman like Ashley would see right through him. Her eyes were too deep, too intense. She'd figure out his secret in no time and realize that he was a man who couldn't stand up to the pressure of his job without breaking into panic attacks.

No. He couldn't afford to daydream about impossible situations. He needed to focus on work and saving patients. Nothing else. That's exactly what he'd do, after he made sure that Theresa didn't view Ashley as a threat to be demolished.

CHAPTER 5

Exam room four smelled like lemon cleaning solution, and all traces of vomit were washed away. In record time, probably. Gwen wouldn't have an excuse to fire her today.

She pushed the cart towards the door. It tilted steeply to the side. Her stomach lurched as she dove to catch it before the cart tipped over again. She balanced it upright, then bent down to examine the wheel again. If the wheel stayed attached to the cart through the end of the week, she'd believe in miracles. Ashley bit her lip and shook her head. The true miracle would actually be if Gwen fixed the cart.

She walked to the other side of the cart and gave it a careful tug. Pain shot through her shin as the cart lurched into her leg. She let out a quiet hiss and allowed herself one second to rub her leg. Then, she straightened and backed up the cart slowly, taking smaller steps to avoid hitting her shins again. She gritted her teeth. Once she entered graduate school, she'd never push a cart again. And once she made enough money to cover rent and food each month, she'd leave a big tip for every cleaning person she met.

She gave the cart a harder tug to get it through the

doorway and backed right into a wall. A wall that let out an angry sound. She jerked upright and cringed as her cart tipped over.

"Sorry," she muttered automatically. The mess was huge. The bottle of liquid soap had cracked in the fall and oozed onto her shoes. She lifted up one foot gingerly, then the other.

"Sorry for not doing your job and cleaning my room on time, or sorry for not bothering to look where you walk?"

Ashley took a deep breath and turned to face the human wall. At least the voice didn't belong to Dr. Evans. Unfortunately, it did belong to one of the other doctors. Why couldn't she run into a kind patient or one of the hospital IT workers? They never bothered her.

Dr. Michael Tobers looked down at her. If he stood any taller, she'd have to strain her neck trying to look him in the eyes. Maybe the air was too thin at his height. Maybe he needed more oxygen in order to act like a decent human being instead of a smug, superior being.

Seven minutes, who can't be patient for seven minutes? Arrogant, impatient, controlling people who were too full of themselves, that's who.

In a fair world, self-absorbed narcissists would look ugly. They wouldn't look like they belonged in a calendar of shirtless doctors. Much less be placed in the starring role of that calendar. Dr. Tobers's dark hair, permanent five o'clock shadow, and intense grey eyes were all the female staff talked about for weeks after he started working at the hospital. Even Ashley fell for the gorgeous looks at first.

Well, he usually looked like a fashion model for hospital scrubs. Today, he looked like he had the flu.

A small giggle came from the nurse who stood next to him. She looked at Ashley with an icy smirk.

"Sorry, I'll have this mess cleaned up right away, and you

can have the room." She lifted her foot again. The liquid soap made a loud slurp.

"Who's your supervisor?" He continued to glare at her, barely moving to give her enough space to turn the cart upright again. Apparently, an apology wasn't enough for Dr. Arrogant. Or that nurse, who muttered something under her breath.

"Gwen."

"Any more problems, I'm calling her. I won't have my patients wait because you aren't doing your job fast enough."

Ashley grabbed some towels from her cart and bent to wipe the liquid soap on the floor. At least they couldn't see her face while she cleaned. She'd need the mop bucket to finish cleaning up the residue. The nurse tapped her foot impatiently, inches away from Ashley's face. Weren't nurses supposed to be kind and full of compassion? Finally, Ashley stood up, flung the last few items onto her cart, and straightened her ponytail. Her face burned, but she grabbed the handle of the cart carefully. She gently tugged it past Dr. Tobers while the nurse wrinkled her nose.

Ashley stopped pushing her cart when she got to the cleaning closet at the end of the hall and released the breath she'd been holding. Maybe getting fired wouldn't be so bad. She could start over, in a new job, somewhere else.

She removed some items from her cart and filled up the mop bucket. The fewer items on the cart, the fewer items to pick up each time it leaned too far over. Too bad it meant that she had to clean the rooms even faster to keep up with the clinic's pace and have time to restock the cart.

"Katie! Come here." Dr. Tobers's demanding voice flew down the hall. Ashley backed out of the supply closet and walked back to the area where the liquid soap had spilled, ignoring him.

"Hey, Katie, don't go clean the exam room. Clean this

mess first." He spoke louder, with a demanding tone. Ashley looked at him. That nurse—Theresa?—still stood next to him, like a shadow. The smug look was still fixed on her face.

"Are you talking to me?" She tried to sound confident, but the words came out in a squeak.

"Your name is Katie, isn't it?" Sarcasm dripped from Dr. Tobers's words. "You have a mop, and there is spilled coffee on the floor. Yes, I'm talking to you. This needs to be cleaned up."

Ashley frowned and grabbed a paper towel. She made her way to the small puddle of light brown coffee, obviously caused seconds ago by either him or the nurse. Didn't really matter who spilled it. They were both too lazy and self-absorbed to clean up after themselves or ask politely for help.

If only they were stuck on that deserted island. Dr. Tobers would be one of the first people running to her for help cooking. He probably didn't know the first thing about cooking or doing anything else for himself. Dr. Tobers and Dr. Evans probably had an army of people at their disposal, people to cook, shop, and clean their houses for them. Sure, they were cardiologists, but put them in a place where they'd have to take care of themselves, and they'd melt under the pressure. By the end of the second day, Dr. Tobers would beg for her help.

And she would help him, but only if he remembered her name.

CHAPTER 6

That evening, Ashley dropped her purse on the small, rickety table by her front door and kicked off her sneakers. Her stomach grumbled as she flipped through the stack of bills that came in the mail. At the bottom of the pile was a thin white envelope from one of the colleges where she'd applied. Her heart dropped.

The next few minutes would reveal if her dreams were finally coming true, or if she'd face another massive stop sign on her path to somewhere better.

Ashley closed her eyes. Her shoulders ached from tugging that stupid cart all day. Everything that could go wrong, did go wrong. She even had to skip her lunch break since Jean never showed up for work. She didn't need any bad news. She just wanted to take a nice hot shower, wash off the grime from the day, and then watch her favorite cooking competition show.

Her eyes stung while she opened the seal to the envelope and withdrew the paper.

. . .

Ms. Hagerman,

We regret to inform you that your application has not been accepted . . .

Ashley crumpled the paper and threw it to the floor. She stomped on it. Hard. Pain shot through her heel. She didn't need to read the rest of the letter to know what it said. *There were too many qualified applicants this year, and we couldn't accept all . . . We encourage you to apply again next year . . .*

It was all lies. The type of lies you tell someone to soften the blow. If the colleges were honest, they would have written, *You'll never be anything more than a housekeeper. You are not good enough.*

One more envelope waited for her. Without looking to see who sent the letter, she opened it and pulled out another single sheet.

Ms. Hagerman, apartment unit 304:

This is official notice that your current lease expires in 45 days. You have the option to renew your lease at the new rate listed below or to give us notice that you will be vacating your apartment at the end of your current lease.

Ashley's head started to spin. The new monthly rate at the bottom couldn't be true. Wasn't there some type of law prohibiting rent increases of more than a certain percentage? How could she possibly afford that price without going bankrupt?

At least now she wouldn't have to worry about getting into graduate school. Finding an affordable place to live would be enough of a challenge.

She crumpled up the letter and threw it against the wall. Who cared where it landed? She'd eventually find it when she packed up all her belongings in a little over a month from now. An evening at home, watching reruns on tv now sounded depressing.

She blinked hard and rubbed the side of her neck. She would fight. She just needed a plan, and then everything would work out. She could figure out something.

She picked up her phone and typed out a text to her cousin Emily.

Meet me at the bar in an hour? Should still be happy hour. More bad news today.

Ashley bit her lip, still staring at her phone. What now? Was there a button to go back in time to this morning? Or to three years ago when she started working in the hospital?

No, if there were a way to go back in time, she'd travel back at least five years, before the car accident that killed her parents.

There was no reply yet to her text. Ashley marched to the shower. Maybe the hot water would wash off some of the bad luck following her. After that, she'd figure her way out of this mess.

CHAPTER 7

The alarm on Michael's phone started beeping. He tapped the screen without breaking focus on the computer screen. Quiet footsteps approached his desk.

"Who uses an alarm to go home? Normal people just leave at the end of the day."

Michael didn't need to look up to know who spoke. "Normal people don't become cardiologists. Normal people don't have others depending on them to save their lives."

"Lots of normal people save lives and go home at the end of the day. Firefighters, police, nurses, even some doctors. Let's go."

Michael tried to brush off his friend again. "Go away. I'm busy."

"I'll wait."

It was pointless to argue with Bill. He learned that lesson years ago.

"It's going to take me longer to finish if you stare at me."

Bill sat down on the dark grey couch along the back wall of Michael's desk. The couch was the perfect size for late-night naps when he worked on the more difficult cases.

Fortunately, tonight was not going to be one of those nights. But that didn't mean that he could abandon his work, half-finished.

Bill stood and grabbed the small basketball on the floor next to the couch. Michael tried to remain focused as soft bouncing noises came from the direction of the mini basketball hoop hanging on his office wall.

Thump. Michael returned his gaze to the chart in front of him and made a few marks. *Thump-thump.* His friend counted in an exaggerated whisper, each number followed by the thump of the small ball. *"Five"—thump—"Six"—thump—"Two pointer! Eight"—thump—"He shoots, he scores!"*

Michael knew Bill's game. He could finish his work in peace as long as he could ignore Bill long enough.

"Did you ask out that cleaner yet?"

He gritted his teeth. "No."

"What's her name? Amy? You should just ask her out."

"It's Ashley. And I don't have time to date."

It didn't make sense that Bill could be as successful as Michael but still have time for an active social life. Even back in their medical school days, Bill always had more free time for relationships, romantic or otherwise. Not like him. How long had it been since his last date?

"Heads up!"

Michael looked up a split second before getting hit in the face with the ball.

"You did that intentionally!" Michael stood up and chucked the ball at Bill. Bill jumped to the side.

"Guilty. Now let's go. You aren't going to be a help to any of your patients if you are overtired and overworked. Balance, friend. Let's head out, have some food and drinks."

Bill was not going to give up at this point. Michael gave him a glare before turning off the computer.

"If I'm going out with you, you need to give me an

opinion on this case. Seventy-four-year-old male, congestive heart failure in early stages, came in this morning feeling weak. Started vomiting in the exam room. I had him admitted for the next few days until we can see what's going on. Lab work showed that he has the flu, and all other results were normal. But I can't help but think that something more is wrong, that the flu symptoms might be masking something more serious." Michael filled Bill in on the other relevant details of the case.

Bill concentrated on the information as they walked out of the hospital and towards their regular bar and restaurant two blocks away. After asking other details about the case, all of which Michael had already memorized, Bill smiled. "Well, doctor," he said with a fake British accent, "sounds like you covered all the bases. I can't think of anything I would have done differently. If something more serious is happening, you'll pick up on it in the next few days. Now, no more work talk. Let's relax."

Michael and Bill entered the busy bar and managed to find a table near the front. Danica, their favorite waitress, appeared at their table as soon as Michael sat.

"Well, if it isn't Dr. Sexy himself!" Danica pulled a familiar magazine from the large pocket in her apron. "Says here that you are still single. Why didn't you tell me that? I could fix you up with someone. Too bad I'm old enough to be your mother." Danica's southern drawl made her sound innocent, but she was fierce when it came to setting up people. How many times had Michael managed to avoid her matchmaking efforts? Normally, Michael managed to brush off her attempts, but she had a particularly focused gleam in her eyes tonight.

Sure enough, Danica slapped the magazine highlighting Michael as a sexy bachelor on the table, mimicking Dr. Evans's same action that morning.

"Danica, great idea. I've been trying to set him up, but he won't go for anyone I choose." Bill scanned the room.

"Don't go looking at that table, Bill. The one woman is married, and that other one is a snob. Not good enough for Michael. She never tips and is always rude. Don't like the service, then don't come here. Don't take it out on me," Danica rambled.

"What about them?" Bill pointed to another table.

"Danica, can you grab me a beer? Any IPA you have on tap." Michael gripped the menu and held it in front of his face.

"You'll get your drink soon, Michael. Just give me a minute." Danica continued scheming with Bill. "There's a table towards the back, two women. They come in here regularly. Only one has a ring, but the other might be single. She's really nice, both of them are, actually. But you stay away from the engaged one, Bill." She crossed her arms and narrowed her eyes at Bill.

"Danica, first of all, I have no problems getting women. Second, I don't ever go for women who are already in a relationship. I can always find a single lady."

Michael noticed that Bill slightly tensed as he spoke. Bill's ex-fianceé had cheated on him during medical school. Since that time, Bill never tried to date anyone who was already in a relationship.

"Let me get you boys some drinks and food. You both want your regular orders? I'll check out the table in the back and make sure the one lady is single."

Before he could respond, Danica picked up the magazine and walked away in one quick motion.

Michael turned to his friend and placed his elbows on the table, leaning forward. He needed Bill's full attention. "About that article . . . the cardio chief is on my back now. They aren't happy about it. Got a written notice this afternoon reminding me of 'professional conduct' within and outside of the hospital."

Bill laughed. "Come on. I know they get serious up in administration, but there's really nothing they can do. They're all talk, no bite. You are one of the best cardiologists in the city. If they fire you, they'll have a huge problem on their hands. Finding a new cardiologist could take over a year. You are fine." Bill had a point. The hospital had looked for a cardiologist for over a year by the time Michael applied.

"If they find out I have anxiety attacks, they might fire me anyway." He turned his neck to the left, then the right, trying to loosen those muscles. Bill knew about the panic attacks, but it was still hard to say the words.

Bill took notice. "I thought things were getting better?"

"They are. I'm fine when I'm not bothered and can focus. Only thing that really set me off this week was getting ripped apart by Dr. Evans."

"That's good then," Bill said. Michael raised his eyebrows in question. "It's happening less than when you started working at the hospital four months ago."

"Five months, actually."

"Even better. You just need a little more time to settle into the job."

Michael shrugged his shoulders, not convinced. He glanced around the room for something else to talk about, anything else.

Danica approached their table again with two beers, barely pausing as she placed them on the table. "Can't talk now, got a few orders, but I'll come back soon." She gave Michael a wink as she left.

Bill shook his head. "She's taking over as your wingman. I'm afraid to see her moves. She's going to have half the women in this bar giving their phone numbers to you tonight." He paused to take a sip of his beer. "You might as well enjoy your fame as Dr. Sexy while it lasts."

Michael frowned. He didn't want to date anyone in this bar. He knew exactly who he wanted to date, and she wasn't here. And even if she were here, it didn't matter. He wasn't like Bill. He couldn't date anyone he wanted and stay committed to his work. If he had to choose between his personal life and his work as a cardiologist, he'd choose his job. He saved lives. He couldn't throw that responsibility away.

CHAPTER 8

"So let me make sure I understand you. You're on probation at work, got rejected from another graduate school, and can't afford your apartment anymore?" Emily picked at the edge of the menu on the table in front of her.

At least her cousin came to happy hour tonight. Misery loved company.

Ashley nodded. "And I lost my favorite coffee travel mug at work."

"Well, now I know what to get you for your birthday."

"Assuming I have a kitchen to put the mug in. I'm about to be homeless."

"I won't let you be homeless. You can sleep on my couch. You were there for me when I needed you. I'll be there for you."

She watched for a second as Emily fiddled with the fake engagement ring on her finger. Ashley had lost count of how many pies, brownies, and ice cream sundaes she made for Emily in the weeks after she discovered that her ex-fiance had cheated on her for two years. She started wearing the fake engagement ring to shield off men until she felt ready to enter the dating world again, and Ashley didn't blame her.

"What can I get you ladies to eat tonight?" Their favorite server, Danica, walked up to their table with a wide smile on her face.

"Burger for me." Emily placed the menu to the side.

"Same here."

Danica leaned forward towards Ashley and Emily, smiling even wider and talking slightly more quietly. "Did you two see who's sitting up front?"

"No . . ." Ashley raised her eyebrows and looked at Emily. Emily just shrugged.

"Well, I probably shouldn't tell you, because we value the privacy of our customers, especially the famous ones."

Ashley fought the urge to roll her eyes. What famous person would possibly want to come to this bar? It had decent food, but most people came because it was close to the hospital and had cheap beer.

Danica pulled a magazine out of the large pocket of her apron and held it in front of them. A vaguely familiar face stared at her, upside down.

"Who is that?" Emily turned her head to get a better view.

Danica glanced around again as if she were about to share important governmental secrets. Then she slowly sat on the empty seat at their table.

"He's a doctor, a cardiologist," she emphasized slowly, "also known as the most eligible bachelor in this area." Danica placed the magazine on the table.

Ashley turned the magazine around so it was facing her, and slowly read the words *Dr. Sexy* written in large letters below the now-familiar face. Her jaw dropped open.

"Yep, he's handsome, and he's *here right now,*" Danica whispered loudly.

No, no, no, no, no . . .

"Where?" Emily asked, clearly catching Danica's bait.

"He's up front, over there." Danica pointed in an obvious manner, no longer pretending to keep the conversation secretive. "But honey, you're engaged. Let's set him up with your friend here. What's your name? You engaged too?"

Ashley stared at the magazine picture. She tried to move her mouth, but the muscles wouldn't work.

Emily jumped in quickly. "Ashley's not engaged. She's not even dating. And she had a bad day. She could use a hot date."

"Leave it to me. I'll set them up." Danica was out of her chair and several feet away from their table by the time she finished the sentence. The magazine remained on the table.

"Emily! What the—" Her tongue stuck to the roof of her mouth. She didn't even know how to finish the sentence because her brain was frozen or something. She coughed and took a sip of water.

Emily just stared.

"She can't set me up with him. Do you know who he is?" The restaurant must have some back door to the alley she could escape through. Maybe over by the restrooms?

"Some super-hot doctor. You had a bad day. Just have some fun. Let's turn your day around."

"No! He's that entitled jerk who yelled at me this morning because there was vomit in a room for *seven minutes* before I could get in there to clean it up!"

"Please don't talk about vomit when we are about to eat."

"Then he called me Katie and acted like I was stupid for not realizing that he was talking to me. After that, he expected me to clean up his spilled coffee when he was standing right next to a pile of paper towels. Plus, I think he was the one who complained to Gwen and got me put on probation. He's the worst kind of doctor, arrogant and conceited and pompous and—"

"Walking this way right now."

Ashley's mouth went dry. Sure enough, barely two tables away, Danica was simultaneously pushing and pulling Dr. Tobers in their direction.

Ashley picked up the nearest napkin and started shredding it to pieces.

CHAPTER 9

Michael Tobers stood in front of her. Tall and imposing, as if he hadn't spent the last several hours ignoring her.

Danica already left. She ran away as soon as the damage was done, as soon as she had delivered this self-centered spawn and his groupie.

"I'm Bill," the groupie said. "Nice to meet you ladies. This is my friend, Michael. I see that you already knew his name, though." Bill gestured to the magazine article lying in front of Ashley.

Heat rose on the back of Ashley's neck and spilled over to her cheeks. The stupid magazine. Dr. Tobers would think she was obsessed with him. Never.

She snatched the magazine and rolled it up. She wasn't on hospital grounds. She couldn't get fired now. This pathetic weapon would make a nice thwack against his arm. Might even give him a paper cut. Teach him a lesson or two about how to treat other people.

Except the magazine flew out of her grip, leaving a sting of pain across the pad of her thumb. A thin line of blood oozed out. Emily held up the magazine, mouthed the word *Sorry*, then turned to the men.

"Hi, Bill, nice to meet you." Her traitorous friend handed the magazine to Bill with her left hand, putting her fake engagement ring on full display.

"Is your friend always this quiet?" Bill gestured in Ashley's direction.

"I could ask the same about yours."

Ashley scowled and looked away. It was none of his business if she talked or not. They had no right to walk over to their table, interrupt their conversation, and expect them to roll out the red carpet at their arrival. Not even if Dr. Tobers looked even better in the dim lighting of the bar than under the harsh fluorescent lights of the clinic. Anyone looked better in bars. That's why bar lighting existed.

A sharp throb spread on Ashley's shin. A second throb followed. She snapped her head up and glared at Emily. Whose side was she on? She tried to kick Emily back but only kicked air where Emily's leg should have been. Emily smiled and tilted her head, eyes wide open.

"Mind if we sit?" Without waiting for an answer, Bill fluidly moved to one of the two empty chairs at their table, leaving the one closest to Ashley for Michael.

Michael paused for a minute and glanced over his shoulder. It almost looked like he thought about leaving their table and walking away. He really was full of himself. She didn't ask him to come to the same bar as her for happy hour. He didn't have to get offended because they weren't jumping for joy at his presence. He could at least tolerate talking with them for more than thirty seconds before looking like he stepped in something rotten. He should leave before she had the chance to tell him what she really thought.

Michael must have decided that he could tolerate joining them for a few minutes because he lowered himself into the chair closest to her, his face blank and cold. "Sorry if we are intruding. My friend doesn't always realize when we aren't welcome." He looked at his large, expensive watch.

"Come on, Michael, we'll only be a minute. Besides, why come to a bar if you don't want to meet people, right?" Bill rested his gaze on Emily.

Emily shifted her body so that her chin rested on her left hand, showing off the fake engagement ring again. Bill's grin wavered so quickly that Ashley wasn't sure what she saw. She had to give him credit, though. He didn't look like he had come to the table under threat of death.

"It's not every day that we are graced with the presence of Dr. Sexy." Emily looked at Bill but tilted her head towards Michael.

"You know our names, but we don't know yours."

Ashley fought the urge to roll her eyes. The entire conversation wouldn't be necessary if Michael ever took the time to talk to people who weren't at the top of the hospital's social ladder.

"I'm Emily. This is Ashley." Emily looked at her expectantly.

Ashley didn't say anything. What could she say? *Hello, I'm Ashley. I'm a janitor at the hospital and cleaned all your exam rooms today. We've worked in the same hospital since you were hired five months, two weeks, and four days ago. Sometimes I also clean your office at night. Except for the nights when you fall asleep on the couch. But you have no idea who I am. You ignore me unless you need something. Why would you care about someone like me?*

The two men continued to stare at her. Of all the places they could have gone tonight, why did she and Emily come here? And why was that doctor sitting with her?

"Hi, nice to meet you, Ashley." Her name rolled off his lips casually, with no sign of recognition.

Ashley forced a smile at Dr. Tobers. If she were a betting woman, she'd bet her next paycheck that he'd forget her name again by the time he left the table.

Emily turned to Michael. "I actually work in the same hospital as you. I'm a social worker."

Michael nodded. "I thought you looked familiar." He narrowed his eyes and scratched his jaw. His eyes lit up. "You work with the hospice patients, right? I actually have a patient on my schedule for tomorrow who'll need a referral to you. Do you have a business card?"

Bill held up his hand in protest. "We're off the clock, Michael." He turned to Ashley. "Michael is one of the hardest working doctors you'll meet. Do you work at the hospital too?"

"No." The word flew out of her mouth, louder than she meant. The men and Emily stared at her. She reached for her napkin and ripped off a small piece. "I mean, I uh . . . I work in the hospital across town." She tore off another small piece of napkin.

Emily shook her head slightly and mouthed something that was impossible to understand.

Bill leaned forward. "Which one? I'm at Sacred Heart Hospital, downtown."

Ashley shook her head. "Not that one. I work at . . . um . . . Saint Peter's hospital."

"Isn't that a few blocks away?" Bill furrowed his brow.

"Yes, but . . ." Ashley looked at Emily, who shrugged. "They have a small clinic across town." She tore off a few more sections of the napkin, then glanced at Michael out of the corner of her eye.

His expression had changed. A tight smile spread across his face, and he ran his palms along his legs. Sweaty hands, awkward grin—was this what a nervous doctor looked like?

Somehow, seeing him nervous gave her strength. She

looked up at Emily, who winked and angled her head towards Michael. The message couldn't be clearer. Emily wanted her to flirt. Revenge sounded better.

She smiled as large as she could and leaned into Dr. Tobers but spoke loud enough for Emily and Michael to hear. "So, the article says you 'are a heart doctor because you are interested in anything related to love.' Is that true?"

Ashley felt a small twinge of victory as a muscle twinged in his jaw.

His Adam's apple bobbed as he swallowed. "They just make up the details to sell more magazines."

"Then I guess it's not true that 'he's been single for seven months waiting for the right woman to steal his heart?'"

"That part is true!" Bill interjected before Michael had a chance. "Poor Michael here has been working too hard. He needs a woman to distract him."

"What else did the article say? I remember now." She raised her voice slightly and recited from memory. " 'He often stays awake at night, dreaming about finding his perfect match, someone who will watch romance movies with him and pass him tissues because he always cries during the—' "

"Enough with the article." Michael moved to take the magazine off the table, but Emily beat him to it and placed the magazine in her purse. Michael narrowed his eyes at her, then must have decided that it wasn't worth the battle of getting it back.

Michael crossed his arms and studied the table in front of him, like he expected everyone around him to entertain him while he sat, brooding over life.

Ashley exhaled quickly. "I guess some people have time for dating. I'm too busy. I have goals that do not involve getting married."

Michael perked up and thumped his hand on the table

like he had won a long debate. "Exactly. Bill, did you hear that?"

Bill shrugged. "I disagree. You can always find time for the person you love. Don't you agree, Emily?"

Emily hesitated. "I don't know."

Ashley's stomach sank. She only wanted to make Michael feel awkward, not Emily.

Bill shifted and pointed to her hand. "You're engaged. You can't tell me that you don't think it's important to have relationships."

"Right. I am engaged." Emily touched her fake engagement ring in a move that was visible to Ashley but probably too subtle for the men to notice. "But that doesn't mean I agree. Ashley's busy. She has other things to do with her time."

Ashley mouthed a silent *thank you* to Emily and turned back to the men. Time for them to go. Her cousin had been through too much in the past few months and didn't need random men bringing up all the unpleasant memories. "So, if you'll excuse us—"

Bill's jaw hung open. "You really don't think love is more important than anything else?"

Emily tilted her head and pressed her lips, the way she did when she talked about her ex-fiancé. "Well, yes, but only if it is true love."

Ashley jumped in. "What good is love if you don't have a job? Money? A place to live? Survival is more important."

"Love won't change any of that, but at least you'll have someone to go through the challenges together," Bill countered.

Ashley stole a look at Emily's pale face and made up her mind. She'd make some extra gooey brownies this weekend to eat while they watched movies. Neither of them needed a man to help them with challenges. They had each other.

"Maybe some people don't need the distraction of a relationship." Michael's deep voice felt like a stab in the back. "I agree with Ashley."

Ashley narrowed her eyes and looked directly at Michael. He didn't break eye contact with her. He sat there like he did her a favor by agreeing. Her stomach churned. "I didn't say that dating was a distraction. I would never insult someone by calling them a distraction."

"You said that you were too busy to date. That's the same thing." Michael crossed his arms against his broad chest and tensed his jaw.

"It's not the same thing." She didn't know how it was different, but she wouldn't start agreeing with Michael. "I just have different priorities now."

"So you aren't open to dating right now?"

"Nope. Are you?" She pressed her lips firm.

"No."

She raised her eyebrows and lifted her chin. "Then why were you in the magazine?"

He shifted in his chair and his left eyelid twitched. "I lost a bet to Bill." He said the words quietly, under his breath, like he hoped she wouldn't hear.

"What kind of bet?"

A flush rose up his neck, and he tugged at the collar of his shirt. "A stupid one."

The corners of her mouth crept up. "What was it?" She leaned forward. He looked so awkward that a tiny chunk of ice melted off her heart.

He shook his head and exhaled loudly but then spoke in a quiet whisper. "If I tell you, do you promise not to tell anyone else?"

She nodded and bit her lip. He inched his chair closer to hers, and his leg brushed up against hers. Another sliver of ice chipped away from her heart. She moved her leg away. She wouldn't fall for his charms.

"You have to promise." He spoke to her like she was the only person in the room.

She nodded.

He glanced quickly at Bill and Emily, who were lost in their own conversation. "I lost a bet on the final score of a football game."

Ashley groaned. Normal people watched football. She would not picture him relaxed on a couch like a regular person, watching football. "That's nothing to be embarrassed about."

He inched closer like he wanted to confide his deepest secret. "Bill recorded the game earlier in the week. He knew the outcome. I didn't realize that the bet was rigged until the damage was done."

Ashley let out a short chuckle. "Well, now you are famous. You could date anyone you wanted." Like any of the single women at the hospital.

"That's the problem. I don't want most women. I want someone who doesn't care about my five minutes of fame that came with the magazine article. Someone who . . . well, never mind. I don't have time to date."

"I guess your job takes up most of your time."

He sighed. "More than you'd imagine. I love my work, but it doesn't leave too much time for anything else."

She stared into his eyes—stormy grey with flecks of gold and brown. Deep, captivating eyes, capable of making her get lost for hours.

He cleared his throat and looked at her in a way that would make her toes curl if he'd been any other man. "Why are you too busy to date?"

She tore her eyes away from his. Her partly shredded

napkin lay in front of her. She picked it up and started shredding it again. "I have better things to do."

He leaned in closer. "There's no one you want to date?"

She tore a small piece of napkin and placed it on the table before trusting her voice enough to respond. "No. I'm more interested in keeping my current job long enough to find a new apartment and get into graduate school. I'm going to be a social worker. Those are my priorities. I don't care about anything else at the moment."

He nodded slowly. "Social work . . ."

Ashley stared at her hands. She needed to keep her focus. The man next to her wasn't a gorgeous guy who wanted to sweep her off her feet. He was a wolf in sheep's clothing. He couldn't complain to her boss and then chair her. Unless someone else complained to Gwen instead of him? She gritted her teeth. Even if he didn't complain this time, he still ignored her at work and acted like the only people worth his time were other doctors or patients. It wouldn't come as a surprise if he thought social workers were beneath him.

She wrapped her fingers around the napkin and crumpled it into a ball, her nails digging into her palms. "I know it isn't as prestigious as being a cardiologist, but it's a good job."

He flinched. "I didn't mean that. I take my job seriously, but I couldn't do my work without the help of many other people. Nurses, pharmacists, scheduling staff, housekeeping . . ."

"Housekeeping? Really?" She glared at him as her shoulders tensed.

He nodded and glanced at Bill and Emily, who were deep in their own conversation. He looked back at Ashley, his gaze serious. "Really. I definitely depend on housekeeping."

Ashley frowned. She didn't want to play games. If he finally recognized her, then he should use his words instead of giving vague hints. If he was angry over the amount of time it took her to clean up his exam room this morning, then he could get up and walk away now. She didn't need to waste any more time talking with him.

"You should go."

His mouth dropped open. "I just meant—"

"I know exactly what you meant."

He opened his mouth like he wanted to argue, then closed it. "Fine." He nudged Bill and stood up. "Time to go."

Bill glanced at Michael, then Ashley. He rose slowly from the table.

Michael looked at Ashley again, with an unreadable expression on his face. His eyes looked softer than before, and his forehead had creases. If he were a normal person, she'd say that he looked sad. But men like him weren't capable of getting their feelings hurt. He finally turned and walked away.

Bill glanced at Michael's retreating form and then back at the women. "Uh . . . nice meeting you both." He turned and followed Michael.

Emily turned to Ashley and held out her hand. "Bill asked me to give this to you."

She looked at the wrinkled napkin and saw black scribbles—a phone number written below Michael's name.

He really took his wingman job seriously.

Ashley picked up the napkin and tore it into small pieces before looking back at Emily. "Let's eat."

CHAPTER 10

Michael stepped through the doors to the inpatient unit and checked his watch. Twenty-eight minutes behind schedule. He sped up his pace and walked around the intern who stood in the middle of the hallway. If he couldn't stay focused, he'd be here all night.

He lifted his chin quickly and pasted on a smile for the nurse at the front counter. "Erica, welcome back. How was your vacation?"

She glanced up from her paperwork. "I wondered when you'd make your way up here. Running late?"

His face stiffened, and he strained to keep his smile casual. "Just a little behind schedule. Any urgent cases this morning?"

"No." Erica raised her head, flipping her hair over her shoulder the same way Ashley did when she wore it loose. He shifted slightly and stuck his hands in his pockets.

"Alright. I'll check in before I leave the floor."

Erica nodded absently and returned her focus to the paperwork in front of her.

Michael plodded to the end of the long counter before his

feet stopped working. He glanced back at Erica, absorbed in her work like he should be.

He hesitated, then glanced down the hall. A patient shuffled slowly down the length of the hall, with a nurse walking alongside for support. Someone else, probably a family member, filled a reusable bottle at the water cooler. There were no cleaning carts or other signs of cleaning staff.

Erica cleared her throat behind him. "Is there anything else you need?"

He shook his head. "No, just . . . do you know . . . umm, who is . . ." He cleared his throat and adjusted the stethoscope around his neck. "Never mind. I-I'll see you later." He took off down the hall before he wasted more time thinking about Ashley.

Michael entered the first room and pulled out the printed list of patients from his pocket. *Henry Velm, age 74, congestive heart failure, admitted yesterday morning.* The vomiter. Michael gave Henry a few tests, which all came back negative. Until Michael knew the cause of his symptoms, he'd need close monitoring. Worst case scenario, his symptoms were related to worsening heart failure.

Henry lay in bed, awake when Michael entered the room. Henry lifted one trembling hand in greeting.

"Henry, how are you feeling?"

"Not too bad. Think I can go home today?" He spoke with a strong voice, which didn't match his appearance.

"Maybe," Michael mumbled noncommittally as he looked at the computer monitor next to Henry's bed. He opened Henry's chart and most recent lab reports. After a long pause, Michael glanced at the older gentleman.

"I'm not thrilled with all of your lab work. I don't think anything too serious is going on, but I want to keep you here another day or two. I'm ordering an EKG for this afternoon and a stress test tomorrow morning."

Michael removed his stethoscope from his neck and positioned it to listen to the man's heartbeat. Slightly irregular.

Michael stepped back and stared at the older man. "If anything changes, if you start to feel any different, tell the nurses, and they'll page me immediately." Michael placed his stethoscope around his neck and turned towards the door.

"Alright, thanks, Dr. Love." Michael stopped and turned back to Henry, who grinned broadly from his hospital bed.

He sighed. "So you saw the article too?"

"Three nurses showed it to me yesterday, and another one showed it to me this morning. You are quite the talk around this wing. People are taking bets on who you'll date next."

"People here have too much time on their hands if they are talking about my dating life."

"Take it from me, doctor. If a nice woman comes your way, give her a chance. Don't get caught up in all the attention from all the women who read the article, women who are only interested in looks and money." Henry coughed.

Michael tried to suppress a groan. Unsolicited advice should be against hospital rules.

"I know, you didn't ask me, and this is none of my business. However, my wife and I celebrated fifty years of marriage, so I might just know a thing or two about relationships. If you're smart, you'll want to hear what I have to say."

Michael took the bait. Hopefully, listening to the old man now would save him from getting an even longer earful next time he stopped by the room. He sat on the edge of the visitor chair and leaned forward. "Alright, let's hear it."

Henry grinned and pressed the button to raise the top half of his bed until he reached a sitting position. "First, all the women around here are talking about you and how to get you. That shouldn't come as a surprise. Believe it or not, I was once a lady's man. Lots of women chasing after me."

Henry laughed as he traveled down memory lane. Michael waited.

"You have to be patient, though. I met my wife at the post office, of all places. Started chatting with her in line. She had wit. Charm. Something about her that I couldn't describe. I couldn't stop thinking about her after I left the post office. Before you know it, I asked everyone around town about her. Took me three weeks to track her down again. Once I did, I wasted no time asking her out on a date. She said yes before I even finished asking. Turns out, she couldn't stop thinking about me either." Henry paused for breath. Michael passed him a glass of water. After a long sip, Henry continued.

"That's the kind of woman you need to look for. There's lots of great women out there, and many of them might chase after you, especially now that you are Dr. Love." Henry grinned, emphasizing Michael's new nickname. "Focus on the woman who gets under your skin. The woman you can't stop thinking about, no matter how hard you try. Don't settle for less."

Michael stood and patted the man's hand. Hopefully, he had listened long enough to satisfy Henry and avoid any additional lectures on how to lose focus at work and watch his career go down the drain. "Push your call button if you start to feel worse or have any new symptoms." He stood up and walked to the door again.

"Ahh, you young ones never listen. But that doesn't mean I'm not right." Henry coughed again as he spoke.

Michael turned to give the older man one last look. He didn't like the sound of his cough. He was going to have to speak with the nurses and have them keep a close watch on Henry for the rest of the day.

CHAPTER 11

Ashley dug her feet into the polished floor and yanked back on her cart seconds before ramming into the broad, muscular chest of Dr. Michael Tobers. The cart jeered sideways and tipped—that stupid broken wheel. If Dr. Tobers complained about this, Gwen wouldn't care that the accident could have been prevented if she'd listened to Ashley and fixed the cart.

He shouldn't even be on the unit now. He should have left fifteen minutes ago.

Her heart started racing. Maybe he wouldn't recognize her. She crouched down to grab the empty bucket and box of garbage bags that had fallen to the floor. She reached up with her other hand and yanked the elastic holding her hair in a ponytail. The elastic snapped, and her hair fell over her face.

She glanced up through her hair. He hadn't moved.

"Sorry," she mumbled. Maybe he would walk away now. He never paid her any attention before, so today should be no different. What were the chances that Gwen would fire her if she pulled the hospital fire alarm?

She started to feel lightheaded. She placed one hand on the floor for support and the other on her forehead.

Maybe he'd leave without seeing her face. Maybe he wouldn't realize that they sat at the same table at the bar yesterday. Even if he did, maybe he wouldn't humiliate her. Maybe he wouldn't accuse her of lying to him last night or laugh at her for thinking that a doctor could be interested in someone who, well, cleaned toilets for a living.

He muttered something quietly. Why hadn't he left yet?

She cleared her throat and tried to speak clearly. "I've got this. Things fall off my cart all the time. I'll get it cleaned up and be out of your way." *Go away, go away, go away.*

He crouched down next to her and reached for the boxes of tissues that had fallen off the cart.

That smell again. Spicy, with a hint of something else. Something woodsy, earthy. He was close. Too close.

"You don't need to help. I can get this." She took a big inhale and reached for something, anything.

Her hand made contact with a box. And his hand. A small shock went through her.

She pulled back quickly. Too quickly. She let out a gasp as she lost balance, fell sideways, and landed with a thud. A dull ache grew in her hip.

"Hey, are you ok?" He didn't sound like a self-centered snob.

She glanced at him out of the corner of her eye.

He held out his hand.

"I'm fine. I got this. You can go away." She bit her bottom lip and stared at the floor. He was actually being helpful. It would be so much less weird if he mocked her.

He let out a soft laugh that sent shivers down her spine.

Great. Was this his plan? Act like a decent human being and then mock her once she let down her guard? Her face was starting to burn.

He placed his hand on her shoulder. "I know you can get this. I just thought I'd help. Need a hand standing up?" He still sounded friendly, the same way he sounded around his patients. Her stomach dropped. He probably thought of her as a patient right now since she fell and could be hurt. No wonder his patients rated him highly on feedback questionnaires. His voice could melt anyone's heart when he acted like a caring person.

Ashley bit her lip hard and glanced around the floor. She needed to maintain her focus. She wrapped her fingers around an unopened box of gloves and threw it on the cart. The moment of truth had arrived. No way to keep hiding on the floor. Time to stand up and hope he didn't cause a scene.

He offered his hand again. She took it and closed her eyes briefly. His grasp felt good, like the calm before a tsunami.

She stood and faced him, flipping her hair behind her shoulder. The tall man standing in front of her exuded confidence, strength, power. Her cheeks grew hot as she stared at his broad jaw with a hint of dark stubble. The same eyes that looked at her curiously the night before were now narrowed and focused. She had no idea what thoughts were going through his mind.

Ashley inhaled deeply. She let go of his hand and turned to her cart.

"Thanks for the help. I'll just . . ." She let the sentence trail off. His eyes didn't show any sign of recognition from last night. She pointed to his hand. "Can I have the tissues?"

He looked down as if surprised that he held the box. He tossed the box from one hand to the other. "I'll keep this box. I'm, um, running low on tissues in my office."

"Whoever is cleaning your office tonight can replace them."

"No, that's ok. I'll just keep these."

Ashley frowned.

"You worked in the clinic yesterday, right? I meant to tell you—" He glanced over Ashley's shoulder and stopped talking mid-sentence. She didn't care. He'd already said enough. He didn't need to finish the sentence to send her the message. He complained to Gwen, Gwen put her on probation, and now she could count on being fired by the end of the day for assaulting him with the cleaning cart.

She scowled and turned her head to see why he continued to stare over her shoulder. Theresa jogged over, looking perky and gorgeous, like always.

She should have run away without her cart when she had the chance. Mean wasn't a strong enough word to describe that woman. If anyone should be placed on probation, it was Theresa.

Her voice came out in a high-pitched tone. "Dr. Tobers, I'm so glad I found you. A few of the nurses were going to order lunch today, and I knew I just had to find you and see if you wanted to order too. What kind of person would I be if I let you forget to eat? I'm not interrupting anything, am I?" Theresa's eyes narrowed as she glanced back and forth between Ashley and Dr. Tobers.

Dr. Tobers rubbed the back of his neck and turned to face Theresa. "Thanks for the offer, but I'm not interested in ordering lunch today. If you'll excuse me, I have patients to see." He gestured for Theresa to move out of his path, but she made no motion.

"Is she bothering you, Dr. Tobers?" Theresa tilted her head towards Ashley and spoke in a loud whisper. "I can call housekeeping and report her if you want. She should know better than to interfere with the doctors."

He shook his head. "There's no reason to file a complaint. I needed tissues." He held up the box for Theresa to see. He turned to Ashley. "Thanks, A—hmm, what's your name?"

Ashley clenched her jaw and pointed to her name tag. "Ashley."

"Right. Thanks, Ashley." He turned back to Theresa. "Let's walk back to the clinic together. I changed my mind about ordering lunch."

Theresa gave Ashley one last look, her nose turned up as though she smelled something rotten. Finally, Theresa and Dr. Tobers walked away together, leaving Ashley by herself.

CHAPTER 12

What an arrogant bastard! Ignores me for months, hits on me at a bar, and still doesn't even recognize me. Talk about a stereotypical elitist, entitled man. Like to see how he'd react if the positions were reversed. "What's your name?" Really? I'm wearing a large name tag, and I work with you all the time! You would know that if you ever pulled your head out of your—

"What did that garbage bag do to you?" A quiet voice broke into Ashley's thoughts. She jumped and looked down at her hands. Her knuckles were white from the death grip she had on the bag of trash. She shoved it in the large garbage bag hanging from her cart before turning to the speaker.

The elderly man lay in his hospital bed, his pale face nearly blending in with the white bedsheets and pillows. His white hair further contributed to the camouflage effect. He reached towards the movable tray near his bed but couldn't touch the items assembled on them. He looked in Ashley's direction. "Help an old guy out?"

"Of course." The tension in her shoulders and neck melted as she rushed to help the man, who looked feeble and weak in the bed. The faded tattoos on his arms hinted at a past where he was anything but frail. Ashley moved the table to his bedside, where he could reach all the items.

"Today's not my best day. Used to run a business, and now I can't even get water and my glasses without help." Ashley waited as he placed his glasses on his face with shaking hands. His gaze moved over to her. "I'd guess today isn't your best day either. What's got you so upset?"

Ashley shrugged. "I really shouldn't bother you with my problems. You need your rest."

The old man smiled. "Honey, I'm bored as can be here. You'd be doing me a favor by chatting with me. Sit. The cleaning can wait."

Ashley looked at the clock and then back at the elderly man. Gwen would throw a fit if she caught her chatting. She sighed.

"Alright, I have a few minutes. What do you want to talk about?" She pulled a small chair up to the side of his bed and took a seat.

"Let's hear the story. Who put the bee in your bonnet?"

Ashley raised her eyebrows at him.

"You millennials. That means, why are you so mad that you were about to use your mop as a weapon?"

Ashley's mouth curved into a small grin against her will. She ran her hand through her hair. "Have you ever felt like people ignore you? You could be standing there, and they never notice you because they think they are better than you?" The words flowed out of her mouth, uncontrolled. "I've seen him at least four times a week, every week, for the past five months. He doesn't even notice me until last night at a bar, but then still doesn't recognize me today! He's just too arrogant to notice me because I clean, and he thinks he's better than me."

She stopped abruptly. Did she really just blurt all of that to an old stranger in a hospital bed?

He looked at her with a knowing gaze. "So this is about a man. How long have you liked him?"

"No, I don't—it's not like that," Ashley stammered.

"So you are just mad because he doesn't know your name?"

"I'm mad because he ignores me and treats me like I'm not as good as he is."

"This guy your boss?"

Ashley shook her head.

"What does he do here?"

"He's a doctor." Realizing that Michael might be his doctor, she ducked her head and quickly added a small lie. "On a different floor."

"Well, sounds like you have to get his attention. Make it impossible for him to ignore you. If you like him, it's worth the work to show him that you can't be ignored."

Ashley considered his words. "Wait, I don't like him. I hate him."

The elderly man reached for his water, taking a prolonged sip before turning his attention back to Ashley.

"Do you know what's on the lunch menu today?"

Ashley looked at him quizzically. "No, sorry, do you want me to ask the aide?"

"Which aide is on duty today?"

"I don't know. I can ask."

"That's alright. Who's bringing my lunch tray today?"

"It will be one of the cafeteria workers. I don't know who."

"So you don't know the names of everyone who works here?"

"No, of course not."

He didn't respond.

Ashley waited a second. "Ok, so I can't expect him to know everyone's name either. But I see him almost every day. He should know my name by now."

He raised one eyebrow and paused. Ashley pursed her lips and drew a deep breath in through her nose. She'd fallen right into his trap. The smug look on his face gave away his intentions. "What's my name?"

Ashley stared, trying to recall.

"You came into my room three times yesterday, once today, and we've chatted for a while. You must know my name by now."

Ashley hung her head. "Sorry, I should have asked."

"It's Henry. Nice to meet you." He held out his hand in a friendly handshake. His hand was cold, frail in hers. "If he's a doctor, he's probably focused on caring for his patients. Find a way to make him notice you. People are always going to ignore us if we let them. Don't blame him if you are willing to let yourself be ignored."

Ashley sighed. A dull headache started to form behind her eyes.

Henry's advice would have been good if he was right about her feelings, but he was wrong. She didn't like Michael. This was not a case of unrequited love.

If anything, this was a case of social class snobbery. Michael thought he could treat others as inferior because they weren't doctors. Michael believed that she wasn't worth knowing because she cleaned the hospital. He'd soon find out that she wouldn't be ignored any longer.

CHAPTER 13

Ashley adjusted her hair one last time in front of the deserted locker room mirror. If she didn't get moving, she'd have to stay late to finish cleaning the cardiologists' offices tonight. Her stomach rumbled in protest against skipping supper, and she frowned at her reflection. She should have grabbed something to eat from the cafeteria before she spent all that time putting on makeup. She brushed her hands over her cleaning scrubs. They weren't wrinkled, but they definitely weren't flattering.

Hopefully, Michael had a hidden fantasy about women wearing hospital-issued cleaning scrubs.

Who was she kidding? She would never be the type of woman men found irresistible and impossible to ignore. But that didn't matter. The old man was right about one thing: she wouldn't let the world ignore her anymore.

First, she'd deal with Michael. By the end of the night, he'd know her name. Well, he might already remember her name from that morning. But after this evening, he'd never forget her. She'd tell him what she thought about him. He couldn't get her fired for speaking her mind. Besides, maybe tomorrow would be the day she told Gwen what she thought about her, too. Then she'd quit this miserable job and get a better one. If graduate school didn't want her, there still must be something she could do. Someone, somewhere, must be interested in hiring someone with years of cleaning experience listed on her resume.

But first things first. Look hot, flirt with Michael tonight, and make him fall for her. Or at least get him to ask her out so she could look him in the eye and tell him all the things she'd rather do than go on a date with a pompous, vain doctor with gorgeous eyes and ripped muscles.

Teach him how it feels to be ignored.

Ashley left the locker room and walked to the supply closet. A door slammed in the distance as Ashley grabbed her cart and dragged it out of the closet. She glanced at the other cart for a second, then turned back to her own. She could handle her own cart for a few more hours. Not worth the risk to borrow someone else's and get in trouble. The bent bracket still held the wheel in place, barely.

Butterflies rose in her stomach as she forced the cart down the long hallways until she reached the wing with the cardiologists' private offices.

As usual, most of the office doors were closed and the lights off. All but one. She grinned. Perfect timing tonight, just as planned.

She stepped up to his office and knocked gently.

Silence.

She opened the door and frowned.

No trace of work remained on the surface of his mahogany desk. The door to the private bathroom was closed, silent as an abandoned cave. She ran her eyes around the large room. A white jacket hung from a lone hanger on the wall, with no signs of its owner.

A lump the size of the wadded paper on the floor next to

his desk formed in her throat. All this effort for nothing. Changed shifts with Kelly, missed dinner, and wasted good makeup for an evening of cleaning alone.

She shuffled to the recycling bin, carried it over to the cart, and dumped the papers into the larger recycle bin on her cart. She let the smaller bin fall to the ground with a quiet thud and kicked it. The bin rolled over itself twice before coming to a stop. She closed the gap and kicked it again across the thick, lush carpet. His office had better furnishings than her house.

She pulled back her foot to kick his recycle bin one last time and stopped. A new dark spot stained the carpet next to his desk. She crouched to the floor and reached out a finger. Spilled coffee. That man needed a lesson on how to carry coffee without spilling it everywhere.

She walked to the side of the cart where the vacuum was lodged between cleaning supplies and the trash bin. One treatment with the carpet stain remover followed by a pass of the vacuum should remove that mark. She clutched the handle of the vacuum and tugged. An avalanche of cleaning supplies broke loose and crashed to the floor. Ashley stepped backward, caught her foot on the vacuum, and landed on the floor with a thud.

Ashley closed her eyes and grimaced. When she was a teenager, her mother said that she'd outgrow the clumsy phase. Why couldn't that day finally arrive?

She cracked open her eyes and squinted at the mess around her. A bottle of hand sanitizer rested next to her hand. She picked it up and threw it across the room. It made a satisfying thunk. She picked up the next item, a large roll of paper towels, and threw that too.

She picked up a roll of garbage can liners and aimed at the empty recycle bin, with one eye closed, picturing

Michael's head. She took aim and threw. "You stupid, son of a—"

Ashley stopped mid-sentence.

She had an audience.

A tall, muscular figure stood in the doorway to the private bathroom. A towel was wrapped around his waist, and his wet hair dripped onto his broad chest. All his ab muscles were on display, and they were even better than she imagined.

Michael.

"Wow. You're here, naked. Oh no, this isn't right." The words tumbled out of her mouth. Was she having a stroke? An aneurism? Did her brain break when she fell? Why was her face so hot?

He furrowed his eyebrows and placed his arms on the edges of the doorframe. "You aren't Kelly."

Ashley stared. He didn't have to look so disappointed. Unless . . . did he have a secret attraction for seventy-year-old women in hospital cleaning scrubs?

She frowned and glared at him. "Of course I'm not Kelly. Why would you think I am? Surprised that you know her name, though. You never remember mine." Shoot, did she say that part out loud?

She jumped to her feet and glanced at him. Maybe he was the one with the broken brain. A vein popped out of his neck, and his jaw twitched. He stared directly at her. She shivered. She couldn't tell what his expression meant.

"Ashley."

"You finally remembered my name. Do you want a medal or something?"

"No, I —"

"Look, I'll just leave this here and come back in a few minutes so you can take off that towel." Her head started spinning. "Clothes. Take off your clothes."

"Take off my clothes?" One corner of Michael's mouth rose, and he looked down, shaking his head.

"No! Ugh!" Ashley covered her eyes with her hand and spun towards the door. Something small moved under her foot, and she lost balance. She hit the floor with another thud. Heat rose from her neck to her eyes.

She blinked hard. She wouldn't cry, not in front of him. She came here to make sure that he recognized her. He needed to see her as a person, not a replaceable cleaner. If he complained to Gwen again—she shuddered. She should have cleaned his office at the end of her shift.

She heard his footsteps as he approached her, but she didn't look over. Warm hands touched her shoulder. "You ok?"

She straightened her spine and wiped her face. If he had an ounce of kindness in him, he wouldn't mention her tears.

"Are you ok? Where does it hurt?"

She turned towards him and inhaled sharply. He crouched, inches away, his dark eyes boring into hers.

Ashley's head spun. The same spicy scent from earlier invaded her nose.

He shifted slightly, and her eyes lowered to his chest. She jolted her head upright again.

"Are you hurt?" He repeated the question again from those firm lips.

She gave the first response that popped into her head. "My pinky."

"Your pinky?" The twitching muscles in his jaw betrayed his serious tone.

"I mean my hand." She hoped the look of pain on her face convinced him. "Ouch." She grasped one hand with the other. She didn't sound convincing to her own ears, but she never went to acting school, and he still wore nothing but a towel.

He reached forward and took her hand. He ran his fingers

over the back of her hand, then turned it over and traced the lines in her palm.

"Does anything hurt when I move your fingers?"

She didn't trust her voice. She shook her head.

He moved her fingers in a few directions. "I don't think anything is broken. If the pain doesn't go away in a few hours, an ice pack will help."

Ashley stared at him, lightheaded.

Michael switched his focus from her hand to her face, raising his eyebrows and giving her a grin identical to the one from the magazine picture. "You do like to make an appearance."

She took her hand back from him. "What do you mean by that?"

His grin disappeared. "Right. Tell you what, give me a minute to put on clothes, and I'll help you clean up this mess." Michael held the towel closed with one hand as he stood up. He walked to the bathroom, paused, and faced her with a searing look. "Don't go anywhere. I want to ask you something."

The door closed with a click before she could respond.

Don't go anywhere? Did he really think that he could throw out commands? She'd go anywhere she wanted. And right now, she wanted to be anywhere except his office.

CHAPTER 14

Ashley walked into the hospital early the next morning, dark chocolate and caramel brownies in hand. She stifled a yawn. She should have picked something more complicated to bake. Something that would have kept her too focused to think about Michael's naked torso.

It didn't work. Once she finally fell asleep, she dreamed of a half-naked Michael making brownies.

She dropped off the brownies in the empty break room, then went to her locker.

A folded piece of paper was taped to the front of her locker. What was this, high school? Whoever left the note obviously never heard of texts or messaging.

She ignored the note and opened the locker as Gwen walked in. "Morning, Gwen."

"Ashley." Gwen's face twisted into something almost resembling a smile.

"Umm, can I do something for you?" Ashley stood up straight and tried to return the smile.

"I'm giving you the chance to redeem yourself for your bad work performance. You can cover Kelly's evening shift today. She's sick with the flu. No overtime, just do your shift and hers. If you actually do the work, I might end your probation earlier than next month."

Ashley stared at her. Extra hours and no overtime pay? Wasn't that against hospital policy or something? Plus, why did Gwen assume she had no life outside of work?

Gwen made an exaggerated motion of looking at her watch, then back to Ashley, frown intact. Gwen probably couldn't keep a smile on her face for more than a few seconds without her face threatening to crack.

Ashley did some quick mental math. Kelly's extra shift would give her a little extra money this month. Not enough to make up for the increase in rent, but it could help get the deposit ready for another apartment. Assuming she could find one.

"Yes, I can do it."

"Fine. Shouldn't you be on the floor, cleaning, by now? You are late."

Ashley looked at the clock. She was supposed to be in the pediatric clinic one minute ago. She sighed.

"Gwen, I'm only running late because you stopped to ask me to cover Kelly's shift."

"Doesn't matter why you are late, Ashley. No excuses, just do your job."

Ashley clenched her teeth and turned to her locker. Gwen needed to relax. Any other person would thank her for covering the extra shift.

Ashley threw her purse in the locker and closed it firmly. The note on the outside of the locker fluttered in the movement, catching her attention again. She grabbed the note and shoved it in her pocket.

～

That evening, Ashley vacuumed a deserted office in the cardiology hall, backing out of the room as she went. She turned off the loud machine once she reached the abandoned hallway and held her breath while she placed it on the cart. She waited until the cart stopped wobbling to breathe again.

She hesitated before entering the next office. Michael's office. She could skip over it and come back at the end of the night, when he'd definitely be gone. Unless he planned on sleeping in his office again. She chewed her lip. She couldn't clean his office while he slept on the couch. And she couldn't skip his office.

She reached out and knocked on the door. No answer. She knocked again, louder, and placed her ear against the smooth wood door. No sound came from the other side.

She grabbed a disinfectant wipe from her cart and lowered to the ground. She wiped the floor in front of the door with the wipe, then laid down, her cheek pressed against the cold, slightly cleaner floor. She squinted to look through the gap under the door. The lights were off.

She stood up and tossed the used wipe on her cart.

She studied the door for a minute, then closed her eyes and reached for the door handle.

The door was locked.

Ashley sighed and grabbed the master key from her cart.

"Hello? Anyone here? I'm just here to clean." Her voice disappeared into the dark room. She crept into the office and flipped the light switch. No sign of anyone in the room. She tiptoed to the door of the private bathroom, muscles tense and ready to flee. Her heart was beating a hundred beats a second, ready to explode.

A deep breath to try to calm down helped a little. She had every right to be here. She had a job to finish. It wasn't like she was trying to break into his office. Besides, anyone within ten feet could hear her heartbeat. She'd make a terrible spy. And she definitely didn't hope for another glimpse of him wrapped up in a small towel.

The bathroom was empty.

Good. She didn't have to see his naked chest again and waste another night lying in bed, haunted by the memory.

Ashley put on her earbuds. She needed to hear something loud, angry, energizing tonight.

She grabbed her cleaning supplies and left the cart in the hallway. She needed to get off probation before the messed-up wheel fell off. Moving to the beat of the music, she started cleaning the office. She walked around the room, performing her meticulous routine. Empty recycling and garbage bins, dust the shelves. She paused at the display case on the far end of the room. Over twenty models of the human heart sat on the shelves, perfectly spaced apart. She glanced around at the other bookshelf, which contained books that were also neatly arranged.

This doctor liked things to be organized neatly and precisely.

She grinned and dropped her dust rag. She picked up one heart model, then another, placing them in a pile on the floor. She wiped the dust from the shelves.

Her skin prickled when she picked up the first model from the floor. She placed it carefully on the shelf. Backward. She grabbed another model, much larger than the first, and placed it so that it nearly touched the first model. She picked up another model and set it farther away. She balanced the next model upside down in its stand.

After a few minutes, she took a step back and admired her handiwork. It looked like a kindergartener arranged the models back on the shelves. Or maybe a toddler.

She made a final adjustment to one heart that looked a little too straight. Too bad she couldn't be a fly on the wall in his office tomorrow morning when he saw his precious heart models all over the place.

A hand tapped her shoulder.

"Ahhh!" Ashley jumped. She grabbed the closest heart model and turned around, ready to attack. She threw the heart at his midsection and put her hands up to fight.

A tall man wearing a white medical jacket over a fitted blue dress shirt stood in front of her. Smirking.

CHAPTER 15

Ashley's face grew hot, and she pulled the earbuds out. "Didn't your mother ever teach you not to sneak up on people at night?"

"I didn't mean to scare you." He raised his hands in a truce but kept the smirk on his face.

"You didn't scare me."

"It sounded like you screamed before you threw that heart at me." He bent down and picked up the heart model by his foot while keeping eye contact with her.

"I was singing to my music and cleaning. It fell out of my hand when I turned around."

"Guess I misunderstood you."

"I guess you did."

She stared at him for a minute. At least he wore clothes. Maybe she could actually focus enough to speak coherently.

He shifted his weight and raised his hand to rub his jaw. "What were you listening to?"

"Nothing really." No point telling him what music she liked. He probably listened to something elitist or intellectual, like Gregorian chants.

She held out her hand to take the heart model back from him, biting the inside of her lip to stop herself from groaning. She shouldn't have messed up his display. It seemed childish and immature now.

He placed the model in her hand, letting his fingers graze hers for longer than needed. Or maybe that only happened in her imagination.

He cleared his throat. "Here, let me help. It looked like you had fun rearranging the models on my shelves. You didn't like the way I had them arranged?"

"No—yes, I mean . . ." Ashley trailed off.

"That's ok. They get moved around all the time. I probably have too many, but I like to collect them. Part of my job, I guess." His hand brushed hers as they both reached for the same model. She held her breath.

He sounded like a normal, nice person. Her stomach churned. He smelled good, too. Intoxicatingly good.

He turned and faced her, voice level and steady. "How's your hand today?"

She released her breath. He didn't feel any spark. Her presence didn't affect him. She needed to control herself. He only wanted to check on her injury from last night.

"It's fine, didn't bother me at all."

"I thought you might have texted me or stopped by my office to let me know. Did you get my note?"

"Your note?"

"I taped it to your locker. Or at least, Gwen told me that was your locker. Don't tell me I put my number on the wrong locker."

She turned back to the shelf and rotated a model. "You didn't put it on the wrong locker. I just didn't read it." She grimaced. "I mean, I didn't have time to read it. Busy day, I had to work late last night to cover for Kelly, and then work my regular shift today and now do her night shift too, and I missed dinner and . . ." She paused and glanced at him. "Now I'm just rambling."

He raised his eyebrows.

She reached into her pocket, stomach fluttering. She pulled out the note and tried to hide its crumpled state with her hand as she opened the page. She read the scribbled handwriting. *How's your hand? Here's my number so you can give me an update.*

Oh. Her legs tensed, poised to run away. He really only cared about her hand. How could she be so naive? They weren't in high school. He wouldn't write something like *Do you want to be my girlfriend? Circle yes or no.*

"Fine. My hand is fine. Here." Ashley held the paper out to him to return his number.

Michael's eyes darkened as he frowned.

Ashley paused, hand still extended. He didn't take the paper.

A lump formed in Ashley's throat.

He was the doctor. She was the cleaner. He didn't recycle the paper for her—that was her job.

She broke eye contact and shifted her weight on her feet. "Never mind. I'll take care of this for you." Not that it would kill him to do an ounce of work for someone else.

He turned and walked to the couch. He ran his hand through his hair before leaning back and settling into his seat.

He looked entirely too comfortable, and he just stared at her.

Ashley cleared her throat, glanced at the door on the opposite wall. She'd never been in a room with him, alone, for this long before. Except for last night, which didn't count because it was too embarrassing to even think about. And why didn't he say anything? Was he going to sit there and watch her while she finished cleaning the office?

She wouldn't put up with this. She deserved better than to be treated as someone's entertainment for the evening.

"I have work to do. I'll come back and finish your office later." She glared at him and walked a few steps towards the door. She paused. She forgot about her wireless headphones, sitting on the shelf next to the model that showed the inner chambers of the heart. She turned around to get them. So much for storming out of his office.

As soon as she touched her headphones, Michael spoke again. "I'll be here awhile. I'm going to order delivery for dinner."

Her stomach let out a loud rumble at the mention of food. She shoved her headphones into her pocket and shrugged. "Fine. Leave the containers in the hall, and I'll pick them up later." She turned around again. He didn't need to remind her how to do her job. The doctors always left food containers in the hall for cleaning staff to pick up at the end of the night. No one wanted their office to smell like stale onions.

"Do you like Thai food?"

"There's a good place on Fourth Street that delivers here. The menu is in the kitchenette." He better not expect her to find the menu for him. He could walk down the hall and get the menu himself or look it up on his phone. She walked toward the door.

"That's not what I meant."

She paused and glanced over her shoulder.

He stood in front of the couch, his lips twisted in a weird way. He tousled his hair with his hand and looked at the wall next to her. "I meant, do you want to order some food too?"

She shook her head. "No." Her stomach growled again, louder than before.

"My treat. As an apology for the other night."

"What do you mean?" Her cheeks grew warm as the image of him standing, in only a towel, grew stronger.

"The restaurant. When my friend and I came over to your table."

She narrowed her eyes and crossed her arms.

He cleared his throat. "I should have said something sooner, I guess."

"I have work to do." She turned back to the door.

"We can order something different. Italian?"

She inhaled deeply, then exhaled. "I'll finish cleaning your office later."

"I heard your stomach growl. You must be hungry."

"It's none of your business if I'm hungry."

"Won't you give me a chance?"

"A chance for what?" The words rushed out, louder than she meant, as she turned to face him again.

He stared at her, eyes dark. "To apologize."

"Fine. Apology accepted. I'm going back to work." She threw up her hands in the air.

"Let me make it up to you. Let me at least explain myself."

She straightened her back and lifted her chin. "I don't need to hear your excuses. I'm not stupid. At first, I thought you didn't recognize me outside of the hospital, which makes sense because you barely acknowledge my existence inside the hospital. Unless you are mad because I don't clean your exam rooms fast enough. I received your message, loud and clear. I'm on probation now, and I really don't want to lose this job. If you are actually sorry, you will leave me alone to clean."

A muscle twitched in his jaw. He ran his hand over the dark stubble. "I recognized you immediately. I should have said so. And I never complained about your work."

She shook her head. "So you deliberately pretended that you didn't know me at the bar. Let me guess. You were too embarrassed to be seen in public with a hospital cleaner? Afraid that someone would see us together? But now that everyone left for the day, you're willing to buy me dinner and talk to me like I'm an actual person." Her heart raced in her chest while her mouth went dry. She studied his face carefully.

He leveled his eyes on her, eyebrows pinched together and jaw tense. The color had drained from his face, and he didn't look as tall as usual. He looked . . . Ashley tilted her head. She couldn't figure out why he'd look hurt.

He fixed his gaze on her and took a few steps to close the distance between them.

"Do you really hate me? Do I really have no chance to apologize? Make things better with you?" His whisper sent chills down her spine.

She lowered her gaze, staring at his broad chest instead of his face.

"I don't see any reason to give you a chance."

He took another step closer, invading her personal space. She took a small step back and bumped against the wall. She closed her eyes halfway, letting out a deep breath, her stomach fluttering. She didn't even like the man, but her hands ached to reach out, grab his arms, tear off his shirt, and kiss him all over. Feel his mouth on her, run her hands through his hair.

He took one last step, closing all the distance between them. She could still leave if she wanted to. Push him to the side and walk out the door.

But she didn't want to.

He looked into her eyes and let out a quiet noise as he placed one hand on the wall next to her head.

"I know who you are. I'm just an idiot sometimes."

"That's a weak excuse."

"I know that you work in my clinic every Monday. You are on the inpatient ward at least once a week, and the patients are always happier after you clean their rooms. I know that you are an amazing baker. I made Kelly promise to give me some of the treats you bring to work each week. My favorite were the strawberry macaroons."

Her head started to spin. She couldn't stop staring at his lips while he spoke. She reached one hand out and tentatively placed it on his chest. His heart pounded against her hand.

"You never talk to me unless you have a mess for me to clean up." She frowned as she spoke but didn't move her hand off his chest.

He leaned his head down in response. "I tried to talk with you. Things get messy, and I don't want you to get in trouble."

"That doesn't make any sense."

"I greeted you in the hall last week, and you dropped your water. We were in an exam room together two weeks ago, between patients, and you spilled your bottle of cleaning solution on the floor. Remember? Soaked my shoes, I smelled like lemon and antiseptic for the rest of the day."

She remembered. He had asked her if she knew of any good hiking paths in the area. She started to tell him about her favorite nature trail when the bottle fell right out of her hand and probably ruined his expensive shoes. She ran out of the room to grab a clean mop. By the time she returned, he had moved to another exam room with a patient. She avoided him for the next two days, which wasn't easy.

He gently put his hand under her chin and lifted it, meeting her gaze.

She searched his eyes. There were no clues of him mocking her. He looked gentle, caring. Her legs felt weak.

"Then there was the broken jar of tongue depressors, the hand sanitizer that spilled all over the floor, the—"

Ashley groaned and looked down. "You made your point. But in my defense, the bracket for the wheel on my cart bent months ago, and Gwen refuses to fix it." She took her hand off his chest, but he shifted and took her hand in his, pressing it back against his chest.

"Wait. I didn't mean to hurt your feelings. I just need to get to know you. Don't go away." He sounded sincere.

Her vision narrowed as the image of Michael and Theresa, standing together, burst into her head. She straightened her spine, reaching her head towards the ceiling. "You say that, but just the other day, you yelled at me to clean up the coffee you spilled when you could have cleaned it up yourself. You also called me by the wrong name."

"I had a bad day."

"Doesn't give you the right to take it out on other people."

"It doesn't. I'm sorry for that. I made a bad decision."

"I need more of an explanation than that if you really are sorry."

He sighed. He let go of her hand, which still pressed against his chest, and tentatively touched her chin. His thumb traced the edge of her jaw. "Dr. Evans went after me for something stupid. He didn't like that magazine article. Then Theresa tried to hit on me. She's not my type. She dropped her coffee, and I used that as an excuse to get away. It wasn't fair to you."

"You called me Katie."

"I did. I didn't want Theresa to know how I feel about you."

Her stomach churned. "Because I'm a cleaner?"

His eyebrows furrowed. "Because she's jealous and would stop at nothing to destroy you if she knew how I feel about you."

A lump formed in her throat, and she swallowed hard.

He lowered his gaze to her mouth but hesitated. "So you'll give me a chance? Even if I don't deserve it?"

She couldn't think with him standing so close to her. She

could only imagine kissing him, over and over again.

She focused on inhaling and exhaling. Kissing him would be a mistake. Men like him didn't fall for women like her. Nothing would change if they kissed. He'd continue to ignore her, she'd regret everything, and she'd have to hide from him in the supply closet during every work shift.

But . . . what if they kissed, he fell in love with her, and all her problems were solved? She'd have someone who cared about her, someone to say hello to in the morning and to eat dinner with at night. For the first time since her parents died, she wouldn't be alone.

She raised her face towards him, keeping one hand on his warm chest, and placed the other on his neck. Dr. Sexy, the most eligible bachelor in the city, could be hers.

He adjusted his grip on her chin and leaned in closer to her. She closed her eyes and moved her hand over the silky smooth fabric of his shirt.

Ashley froze. She had never touched a shirt like that before. It had to be expensive. She turned her head to the side and opened her eyes. The couch across the room definitely cost more than her monthly rent. Several shelves were lined with big textbooks, ones you only get after spending a fortune at medical school. Even his office desk and chairs screamed money.

This would never work.

Michael's lips brushed her cheek. She inhaled sharply, and he jumped back as if he'd touched a hot iron.

"I'm sorry, I thought you wanted this too." He frowned and stepped back. He turned around and started pacing, his hands running through his hair.

Ashley hung her head and walked towards the door. "I'll come back later and finish your office. After you go home."

He mumbled something in reply but Ashley didn't look back.

CHAPTER 16

Michael paced his office like a trapped animal.

What just happened? He thought she wanted the kiss. And like a fool, he tried to give her one when she clearly did not want it.

He had lost his mind. That was the only explanation for his behavior.

Pacing the office wasn't helping. The walls were closing in on him, and the room was getting too hot. He needed to escape before the panic attack set in.

He grabbed his sneakers and walked out of the office, hoping that he wouldn't see Ashley again. He'd be lucky if he wasn't called back in to see Dr. Evans tomorrow for accusations of workplace sexual harassment.

How could he be so stupid as to risk everything by trying to kiss her? At work! His career and reputation would go down the drain if she filed a complaint or told anyone about what just happened. There was no excuse for his behavior. The only thing he could say to defend himself was that he thought she was about to kiss him.

He stalked to the staircase at the end of the hall and yanked the heavy door open. He paused only to change out of his dress shoes and lace up his sneakers. He threw his shoes to the corner and started jogging upstairs.

Had she even said that she was going to give him another chance? He started to jog faster up the steps as he replayed their conversation. She had every reason to be angry with him when they started talking. He should have let her know that he recognized her the other night, and he definitely should have treated her better at work the other day. But those were just two small incidents. They saw each other all the time at work.

His heart was pounding, and he broke out in a sweat as he reached the top floor landing and turned around, ready to jog down the ten flights.

He thought he'd been nice to her all the times he helped her clean up a mess or tried to stay out of her way. Did she have no idea how many times he wanted to ask her what she was thinking behind her deep, serious eyes? How many times he had thought about how to get her away from prying eyes and ask her on a date? How many times he wanted to wrap her up in his arms and forget about the rest of the world?

This was the last time he was ever going to take advice from that patient, Henry. The old man had no idea how far Ashley had crept under his skin over the past two months since he first started taking notice of her.

And now, he had blown all of his chances with her by pretending he didn't know her at the bar.

He reached the third-floor landing and turned around. He needed the challenge, the pain, of running up the steps instead of down.

Was he so consumed in his work that he only made up his attraction to Ashley? How many times had they actually talked, had a real conversation? What did he really know about her?

He ran up and down the ten flights of stairs for another twenty minutes until sweat soaked through his button-up shirt, stopping only when his phone buzzed.

The delivery man was about to pull up to the front of the hospital with dinner for him and Kelly. He'd been so busy today that he forget to cancel their weekly restaurant order.

He jogged down the remaining flights of stairs and went to the main hospital entrance. The delivery car was just pulling up, and a minute later, Michael had his food. He walked back towards his office.

There was too much food for just him. He and Kelly started their routine of Wednesday night dinners together just a few weeks after he started working at the hospital.

If only he hadn't ruined his chances with Ashley, he could be sharing the food with her tonight instead of eating alone.

He approached the entrance to the hallway lined with cardiologist offices and paused. He did not want to make the situation worse by running into Ashley again. On the other hand, maybe if he did see her, she would let him apologize. Maybe he could even convince her not to file a complaint against him for sexual harassment.

No, it would be better to leave her alone. Give her space. Anyway, he deserved to be raked over the coals by Dr. Evans. Months ago, his therapist had reminded him not to jump to conclusions. There was the possibility that Dr. Evans would just give him a formal disciplinary action but not fire him.

He opened the heavy door that blocked the hallway of offices from the main corridor of the hospital and let it slam behind him. He took a few steps into the hallway and then coughed loudly. He stomped his feet for extra measure. Surely, Ashley would hear him and either avoid him or confront him, but at least he wouldn't accidently sneak up on her again.

Her cleaning cart was at the end of the hallway, three doors down from his office. He watched as the office door closest to her cleaning cart closed quietly from the inside.

Message received; she did not want him anywhere near her.

He sighed and walked into his office and turned on his computer monitor to review some charts while eating.

The food tasted like cardboard in his mouth. And he couldn't focus on the chart when his mind kept wondering if the noises he heard were Ashley.

There was no point in staying in the office tonight.

He stood up and looked at the container of food holding Kelly's order. Grabbing a piece of paper, he wrote a short note. But he crumpled it up and threw it away, then grabbed another piece and wrote an even shorter note. *Ordered extra food by mistake, left it in the break room fridge in case you are hungry. Sorry about earlier.*

He grabbed his work bag, placed the food in the break room fridge, and then walked quietly down the hall until he reached the office that Ashley had last been cleaning. Her cleaning cart was still in the hallway next to that door, which was slightly ajar. Michael placed the note on top of her cart, where she would hopefully notice it, and then hesitated.

The door was open about two inches, but it was silent inside. He inched forward and tried to peer inside the crack. He couldn't see anything.

A smart man would have stopped and left Ashley alone. An even smarter man would have realized that he was walking on thin ice. First the unwanted kiss, and now trying to spy on her while she was working.

But he wasn't smart. He was desperate.

No other woman had this effect on him. He'd never spent

weeks thinking about a woman he barely knew. She was right about that. He knew almost nothing about her, only what Kelly told him on occasion. But he'd been very careful about asking Kelly too much about her. He didn't want Kelly to get suspicious. He didn't even want to think of the consequences if rumors started around the hospital that he was chasing after a housekeeper, or any other member of the staff at the hospital.

He didn't even know what he was going to say to her if she caught him trying to catch a glimpse of her before he left.

There was no sound coming from the office. The only sound in the hallway was the thumping of his heart.

He nudged the door gently with his foot, moving it slightly. He did it twice more. There were still no sounds coming from the office.

He opened the door far enough to step in and heard a quiet moan. He scanned the room for the source of the noise.

Lying on a couch, sound asleep, was Ashley.

He should back away before she woke up and caught him staring at her. But she looked cold and vulnerable. He snuck out of the office, walked down the hall to the supply closet, and returned with a blanket.

He carefully placed the blanket on top of her, not daring to breathe. His hands ached to touch her, brush the hair back from her face, or lie down next to her and embrace her while she slept.

That would definitely get him into more trouble than he was already in. No hospital would want him if he was fired for trying to kiss another employee and then watching her sleep. He wouldn't even want to be around himself if he acted like that.

Using all the self-restraint he had, he backed away once again and turned off the light to the office. He closed the door gently behind him and backed right into Ashley's cleaning cart.

"Umph . . ." He groaned in a whisper and grabbed his hip, which had taken the brunt of the force from her cart.

He should have grabbed that stupid cart instead because it toppled over, sideways, from just the impact of his body.

This was great. A bottle of liquid hand soap was leaking onto the floor, and there were no towels to be seen to clean it up. Not to mention that this noise was loud enough to attract the attention of anyone within a five mile radius.

He froze. How was he going to explain this to Ashley? He grimaced, thinking about how her face was going to look when she saw what he did. He might as well say goodbye to any chances he had with her and clear his schedule for the long meeting he was surely going to have with Human Resources and the chief of cardiology tomorrow to reprimand him for his actions.

Unless . . . he dared to turn around again and glance over his shoulder. The light in the office was still off. The only noise was his own breathing. Maybe . . . He gently opened the door a crack, just in time to hear a quiet snore coming from the direction he'd last seen Ashley. Could she actually have slept through that noise? Either she was exhausted beyond belief or just a very heavy sleeper. Either way, this meant that he could still fix the situation.

He grabbed a cloth towel from the cart and mopped up the spilled hand soap as best as he could, which was not good at all. Now there was a film of soap going halfway across the width of the hall, a very sticky cloth towel, and his pants were covered in soap. He turned to the cart and picked up the mop. Maybe that would work better? He glanced around but didn't see a bucket. The mop would probably work alright without the water, though. He started mopping up the hand soap. Now it was even worse than before.

He frowned. Maybe there was something else on the cart to clean up that mess. The cart was still on the floor, and he lifted it by the edge to put it upright again. The cart wobbled dangerously, even while upright. Holding it carefully, he looked at the bottom of the cart. One of the front wheels was almost entirely off the cart, and the back wheel was angled awkwardly. No wonder this cart fell over; it was moments away from falling apart completely.

How did Ashley get any work done with this broken mess? It was hard enough to get it to stay upright on its own. And all along, he'd thought she was the cause of all the spills. He'd thought that she was just nervous around him because she liked him too. He'd read her completely wrong. She wasn't jumpy around him because of any crush. She just had a broken cart, and he was too full of himself to realize that maybe she just wasn't interested in him.

Well, he was just going to have to work harder to show her that he wasn't the entitled doctor that she thought he was.

He reached into his pocket and pulled out his cell phone. Desperate times called for desperate measures. Not that Kelly would mind helping him out, but it could lead to awkward questions about why he needed her help cleaning the clinic in the first place.

Two hours later, Michael did one last walkthrough of the offices. Everything was freshly clean. Well, at least marginally cleaner than it was two hours ago. His back ached, and his arms were tired. How did Ashley do this every day?

He crept to the closed door where Ashley was taking her nap, pulling the cart behind him until it was placed next to the office door. He gently removed any breakable bottles from the cart and placed them carefully on the floor, trying his best to make it look like they had fallen after the cart fell and not placed there intentionally. He cautiously opened the door, barely daring to breathe. With the other hand, he gave a gentle push to the cleaning car.

The cart fell predictably with a loud *crash*. Ashley turned slightly in her sleep but was still asleep. Michael's stomach tensed. He flicked on the lights, and she bolted upright. Michael took off at a sprint to the exit door, letting the door slam shut behind him.

CHAPTER 17

Thursday morning came too early. Ashley managed to survive her shift, but her back, legs, arms, and head ached by mid-afternoon. Avoiding Michael at work took every last ounce of energy. And a lot of caffeine.

By dusk, Ashley parked her car in Kelly's driveway, her trunk full of groceries. Cooking was better than a nap or an extra cup of coffee. Plus, Kelly would know how to deal with the Michael situation. Who almost kisses a guy and then runs away at the last moment?

She parked in the driveway and carried the first two bags of groceries to the front door. She left them there and had returned to the trunk to unpack the rest when a dark, sleek Tesla silently slid up to the curb in front of Kelly's house. She turned, putting her hand in front of her face to see who the driver was.

Kelly hadn't said she was expecting company tonight. Besides, she wouldn't know anyone who drove a car like that. Probably someone had the wrong address or needed to turn around. Kelly lived in a decent part of the city, but it wasn't the type of neighborhood for fancy cars.

She carefully grabbed the last of the groceries out of her trunk and walked towards the door. The Tesla remained motionless, with the driver hidden in the shadows.

She shivered as a sense of dread spread from her neck to her toes. Kidnappers usually used vans, not expensive cars. Unless the kidnapper planned to sneak up on an unsuspecting victim in a safe neighborhood at dusk when people closed their curtains and didn't look out at the street. No one would hear a silent car speed away from the scene of a kidnapping.

She regretted drinking so much caffeine today and listening to the *Real Crime* podcast while shopping for groceries. Why were they so addictive?

Ashley picked up her speed and walked quickly to the front steps. A dog barked somewhere from down the street. She clenched her jaw and ran up the steps to the front door where she shoved the door open and dropped the bags on the entryway floor. Stepping back outside, she quickly grabbed the remaining bags. One bag ripped, sending butter, a head of broccoli, two lemons, and several avocados across the floor in Kelly's foyer. She slammed the door shut behind her and locked the deadbolt.

"Kelly, I'm here, and you really shouldn't leave your front door unlocked like that. You have no idea who might come in!"

She was greeted with silence.

"Kelly?" She glanced around. The podcast she listened to last week started out the same way. Quiet evening, quiet street, then the woman was murdered.

She scanned the entryway. Nothing looked unusual. The entry table displayed a fresh bouquet of flowers and a small lamp, both perfectly arranged. The mirror on the wall was slightly tilted, with its right corner lower than the left. Ashley stepped closer and adjusted it slightly, but the mirror slid back to its tilted position. Ashley let out a breath and relaxed her shoulders. Everything was the way it should be. Everything was safe. Not every evening would turn into a brutal crime worthy of a podcast episode.

She grabbed as many of the grocery bags as she could and marched back to the kitchen, her steps echoing off the hardwood floor. She could only imagine what Kelly would say if she'd seen her race inside. But Kelly never came home to find out that someone broke into her apartment, like some of the victims in the podcast episodes.

She opened the fridge and surveyed the contents, pushing the thoughts about the podcast to the back of her mind. Her hands tingled with familiar anticipation, but cooking was much better when she didn't have to pay for the ingredients.

A faint voice drifted down through the ceiling. "Ashley, is that you? I'll be down soon."

Ashley rolled her eyes. As soon as she had enough extra money, she'd buy Kelly a guard dog. Not one of those cute little poodle mixes that looked like a teddy bear and couldn't scare a flea. Kelly needed the largest dog with the fiercest bark, one that would scare away anyone who would want to harm Kelly. Ashley pulled a few items out of the fridge and froze as the hairs on the back of her neck rose again. She walked over to the glass sliding doors that led from the kitchen to the back porch and flipped the lock.

Back at the counter, she pulled out two pots, a frying pan, and a cutting board. Maybe she could afford a guard dog of her own after she finished graduate school. She'd need something bigger than the dog she had when she was a kid, but not too big. A medium-sized dog would be perfect—one with floppy ears to scratch and who would stay by her side. As long as the dog had a fierce bark, size didn't matter. She could even make homemade dog treats for her future dog.

She'd finished organizing half of the groceries when the

doorbell rang. She jumped, dropping a pint of creamer on the floor. Her hand clutched her chest, and she looked to the sliding glass door behind her. No one stood there. She furrowed her brow and bit her lip. She needed to calm down.

No sound came from upstairs. Ashley picked up the creamer from the floor silently, eyes glued to the kitchen doorway. The doorknob to the front door rattled.

Kelly didn't mention any guests for dinner. This evening really was turning into that podcast episode. The woman was home alone, someone stopped by unexpectedly, broke in, and . . . Ashley shivered.

The person in the Tesla must be a stalker. There could be no other explanation.

Unless Kelly invited over a guest. But she never had guests on Thursday nights.

The doorbell rang again. Kelly's voice floated down. "Ashley, can you get the door, please?"

Ashley squeezed her eyes shut and counted to three. Kelly trusted everyone. She'd invite a group of thieves into the house, make them tea, and give them a tour. That's exactly why she needed a dog who'd bite first and ask questions later.

She grabbed the paring knife from the drawer and straightened her spine before beginning the walk to the entryway, not daring to blink. She kept a firm grip on the paring knife.

She saw a flash of movement through the frosted window next to the front door. If she could see movement, then whoever stood outside the door would be able to see her movements too. She stepped nimbly to the door, clutched the knife by her side, and swung the door open.

Her jaw dropped open.

No, no, no, no, no . . .

Kelly's voice rang out from the hallway behind her. "Michael, come on in!"

He stood on the welcoming mat, the porch light shining on him like he was the leading man in a dream. Or a nightmare. He locked eyes with her.

Kelly stepped next to Ashley. "Do you plan on staying outside all evening? Come in before any bugs enter." She waved her hand in the air, shooing away an army of nonexistent insects.

Ashley stepped to the side and shoved her hand behind her back, hiding the paring knife.

Michael stepped through the doorway, looking only at Kelly. "I picked up some ice cream on the way over."

Kelly stepped forward and enveloped Michael in a hug. "You shouldn't have. But I'll accept it as a peace offering for not coming by last week."

Michael returned Kelly's hug as if it was normal to stand in her entryway, hugging the woman who was old enough to be his mother. Ashley gripped the knife handle harder.

"Couldn't help it. Work emergency." He pulled away, shrugged off his jacket and shoes, placing them casually in the closet by the door.

Kelly crossed her arms. "You work too hard."

"It's the only way I can afford your favorite ice cream." He smirked and held out a cloth grocery bag, which Kelly snatched from his hands.

Kelly peeked inside the bag. "You're forgiven."

Ashley tried to take in the scene unfolding in front of her. This man couldn't be the same man from the hospital. And what happened to Kelly? She took a step backward toward the kitchen.

Kelly looked up from the bag and caught Ashley backing up. "Ashley, sorry I didn't come down sooner. You know Michael, right?" Kelly barely paused to give Ashley a chance to answer. "I've been looking forward to your eggplant parmesan all week. Are you still making it?"

Ashley nodded her head.

Kelly and Michael both stared at her.

She gripped the knife harder and stepped backward again. They still stared. "I, um . . . I bought everything for all the meals this week, including eggplant parmesan. I have the receipt in the kitchen." She glanced over her shoulder.

Kelly clapped her hands together, causing the bag of ice cream to bounce wildly. She turned to Michael. "Ashley is an amazing cook. She comes over each week, and after a few hours, my fridge is full of enough food to last me until her next visit." She faced Ashley again. "You really should charge me more for making my meals."

"You really should stop paying me more than I charge you," Ashley responded automatically with the familiar words, then cringed. She glanced at Michael. He met her gaze. Her stomach lurched and she looked down. "I need to go back to the kitchen."

Kelly narrowed her eyes and stepped closer to Ashley. "Ash, are you ok? You're awfully flushed." She placed her hand to Ashley's forehead before she could stop her. "Michael, what do you think? You're a doctor. Does she look sick to you?"

Ashley brushed Kelly's hand off her head with her free hand and ducked her head. "I'm fine."

Kelly crossed her arms. "You look tired." She gave Ashley the look that always made her feel like a five-year-old child who got caught stealing a cookie from the cookie jar. "How much coffee did you have today? You know how too much caffeine makes you jittery."

Ashley shrugged. "I was tired. Remember? I took over your shift yesterday. You don't look very sick." As soon as the words flew out of her mouth, she felt the blood drain from her face. The almost-kiss from last night. She shouldn't have mentioned anything in front of Michael. She looked back to the kitchen and instinctively reached both hands up to tighten her ponytail.

A loud gasp came from Kelly. "Young lady, what is in your hand?"

A muffled snort came from Michael. Ashley glared at him. The corners of his lips were drawn down, but his eyes mocked her.

She set her jaw and refused to look away first. "I thought there might be a robber at the door."

The corners of his mouth quivered.

Kelly shook her head. "Hmph. You always do that. You drink too much coffee, get all hyped up, and let your imagination run wild."

Ashley pursed her lips. "You trust people too easily."

Kelly let out a loud sigh. "Michael, help me out here. She doesn't think I can protect myself."

He cleared his throat. "I agree with Ashley."

Her mouth dropped open. "What?"

Kelly punched his shoulder playfully. "If you don't have anything nice to say, don't say anything at all."

He laughed. "I've told you a hundred times. You need a guard dog."

Ashley crossed her arms, careful not to stab herself with the knife. "How do you know Kelly?" She stepped closer to Kelly. This woman was her friend, not Michael's. Even though they weren't related, Kelly had stepped in as her mother figure years ago. No one criticized Kelly. She could tell Kelly that she needed a guard dog, and Michael could mind his own business.

His Adam's apple bobbed as he swallowed. "You might say that Kelly helped raise me." The smile disappeared from his face.

Ashley waited a moment, then looked at Kelly.

"It's true. He grew up next door to me. Played with my sons all the time. I even changed a few of his diapers—"

"We should put that ice cream in the freezer before it melts." Michael stepped forward and grabbed the bag from Kelly's grasp, keeping his eyes on the knife in Ashley's hand. Ashley stifled a laugh.

Kelly raised her hands in defeat. "Fine. I'm going to go relax in the living room while you cook, Ashley. Unless . . ." Kelly looked slowly between Michael and Ashley. "Michael, why don't you help Ashley in the kitchen?"

"No." His voice came out firm.

Ashley tightened her grip on the knife handle and turned to him.

His face flushed. "I shouldn't help. I mean, I don't know anything about cooking. All I can make is spaghetti with sauce from the jar. I'd get in your way." His words came out rushed, as though the thought of spending one minute helping her would cause him to spontaneously combust.

Ashley's stomach dropped at the sound of his weak excuse. Last night he tried to kiss her, and tonight he couldn't even bear to spend time alone in the kitchen with her. She made the right choice by walking away from him before they could kiss.

"You two go relax. I'll get you when dinner is ready." Ashley forced a smile which she hoped didn't give away how much she wanted to burn his chicken dumplings.

An hour later, Ashley looked around the kitchen, satisfied. Kelly's granite counters were clean, the dishes washed or placed in the dishwasher. Now, the only signs of the cooking that occurred over the past hour were the casserole and eggplant parmesan baking in the oven, caramel brownies cooling on the counter, a pot of chicken dumpling soup simmering on the stove, and the pasta salad chilling in the fridge.

She set the dining room table for two people and dished out the soup. The soup came out amazing, as always. The broth had a full flavor from the onions, carrots, and celery, and the homemade dumplings were perfectly cooked. Ashley clenched her jaw. Her mother had made her promise to keep the family recipe a secret and only make it for people who were special.

Well, tonight, Michael would try it. If she had known he'd be there, she'd have planned something different. Liver and onions. Something that wouldn't make her skin crawl at the thought of him eating it.

He probably wouldn't even like it. He'd probably think it was made from a can instead of requiring a multi-day process that started with making homemade broth.

Well, if he couldn't even appreciate the finer things in life, that was his problem. Not hers. She planned to head home anyway, so she'd never know what his unsophisticated palate would think of this meal.

She walked to the entryway and slid on her shoes before she grabbed her purse and jacket, then paused in front of the hallway mirror.

Overall, she looked ok. A little lipstick would be nice, or mascara. She rummaged through her purse and found some chapstick. She slid it over her lips. Too bad her purse didn't contain a nicer shirt, one that didn't feature large letters over her chest that stated, Need More Cowbell.

She walked to the doorway of the living room. Kelly and Michael were absorbed in a talent competition show. One contestant stood on stage, singing a country song while spinning a hula hoop around his waist. Ashley covered her mouth to stop the laugh that nearly burst out. She loved this show. Kelly never watched these types of shows. She preferred shows about medical drama. She slid her gaze to Michael, who sat at the edge of his armchair, eyes glued to the screen. She could only see the side of his face, but his mouth hung open, and his head bobbed in sync with the hula hoop rhythm. He pumped his fist in the air when the song finished, and the hula hoop kept spinning around the singer's waist.

She cleared her throat and forced the corners of her lips down. "Kelly—" The words caught in her throat as Kelly and Michael looked at her. She tried to focus on just Kelly. "Um . . . I'm leaving. Turn off the fridge in twenty minutes and put the food in the oven after it cools. I mean—no, the food is in the oven. Put it in the fridge for twenty minutes. I mean . . ." She inhaled deeply and looked at the ceiling.

"Got it. I'll take the food out of the oven and put it in the fridge once it's cool. Dinner ready? Smells delicious." Kelly's quiet voice filled the room.

Ashley glanced at Michael. He stood, hands in pockets. "Dinner's on the table. I'll, um, see you tomorrow, Kelly." She paused. Kelly would kill her if she left without any attempt at good manners. "Bye, Dr. Michael—Tobers, I mean . . . bye."

She turned and rushed out the front door.

CHAPTER 18

The sound of the front door slamming shut echoed in Michael's ears. Michael and Kelly stared at each other. Even across the distance of the room, he could feel the heat radiating from her eyes. He pulled his hands out of his pockets and motioned to the kitchen. "Time to eat?"

"What did you say to her last night?" Kelly's voice cut through him like a knife.

"I didn't do anything." Michael shifted his feet and stared at the decorative cat pillow on Kelly's couch.

"I'm not stupid. She looked like she saw a ghost when you first got here, and you looked even worse. Not to mention that you looked at the doorway every time she walked by."

"I had a hard day and I'm hungry. Why does she cook for you, anyway?"

"Don't change the topic." Kelly stared at him.

He scratched his neck. His own mother didn't make him squirm as much as she did. Even when he was little, living next door, she instinctively knew when he misbehaved. Like the time he was three years old and tried to take a dead bird home from her yard. Or the time he and her youngest son stole the cookies from her kitchen. Or the time they made a skateboard ramp that went from the door of the treehouse, eight feet in the air, to the ground. She didn't even give them a chance to try the ramp before taking it apart. Too bad she didn't stop them in time the next day when they rebuilt the ramp. Michael's leg throbbed at the memory of the fracture he got that day.

Kelly had perfected the art of the parental glare.

"Fine." Michael let out a loud sigh. "She got mad at me last night at the hospital. We fought. We both went back to work. The End."

"You and I both know that is not the end of the story. Why did you fight?"

"It was nothing, really." He held his breath.

She remained silent. Seriously, she should have taken a job as a military interrogator.

"Fine. She was mad because I tried to hit on her at a bar but acted like I'd never met her before."

Kelly frowned and narrowed her eyes. "And . . .?"

"And then I tried to kiss her last night." He couldn't look at Kelly anymore but still felt the weight of her glare.

"Don't tell me that you two are acting like a bunch of middle-schoolers because you have crushes on each other."

"Ouch." He flinched.

"Do you like her?" Her words were clipped but with a gentle edge.

He paused. He couldn't stop thinking about her. She got under his skin and played the lead role in his daydreams. He needed to be near her, but he also needed to stay focused on work.

"No."

Kelly let out a puff of air. "Hmph. You can't lie to save your life."

"I don't have time for dating. You know that."

"There's never enough time for everything. That's why you make time for the things that are important."

He shrugged and pointed to the doorway. "Dinner's going to be cold. Ready to eat?"

"I can't help you if you don't know what you want."

"Fine." He pinched the bridge of his nose. "I like her, but she's made it clear that she doesn't like me."

Kelly waved her hand dismissively. "She's slow to get close to people. But once she does, once you earn her trust, she's a friend for life."

Michael thought over what she said. "What if she decides she can't trust someone?"

Kelly shrugged. "She's been through a lot. I think you still have time to win her over. But don't mess up. I don't think she gives people second chances."

Kelly stood up. Michael's lips burned with questions. Why didn't Ashley trust easily? Why didn't she give people second chances? Did he already waste his one and only chance with her? What would it take to win her over? And what had she gone through to make her so cautious?

He followed Kelly to the kitchen, where an enticing aroma filled the air. Two bowls of steaming soup were on the table, with a basket of bread and water glasses.

His stomach twisted. She spent all that time making the food, and he'd made her so uncomfortable that she ran away. He glanced at Kelly.

She smiled as if she could read his mind.

"I'm going to run to my car to get . . . something."

Kelly raised her eyebrows.

"Fine. I'm going to see if Ashley is still here so I can apologize and convince her to join us. If she won't, I'll leave so you two can eat together."

She grunted her approval. "Don't take too long. I'm hungry."

Michael turned and walked until he passed the front door and stepped onto the porch. The cool, damp porch stung his feet, but that didn't matter because unless he was hallucinating, her car sat in the driveway.

He barely dared to blink for fear that her car would disappear from sight. It wasn't even running yet. He thanked the universe that she had to make a phone call or something before she left Kelly's house.

He inched over the damp gravel driveway to the driver-side window and tapped gently.

CHAPTER 19

"Shoot-shoot-bugger-shoot." Ashley stared at her phone.

A light tap on her window startled her. She released her phone and slammed her hand into the car door. The automatic door locks clicked in response. She looked up and groaned. Michael.

"Are you trying to give me a heart attack?" She rubbed her forehead.

He moved his mouth and waved his hand near his face. Muffled sound passed through the closed car window. She frowned and held up a finger to stop him. The light mist in the air left small water droplets in his hair, which glistened in the glow from the lights of Kelly's house. She bit her lip. She'd never kissed a guy in the rain.

He tapped the window again with one finger. Her breath caught in her lungs as she realized what he wanted. She placed her key in the ignition and turned it enough to roll down the window. The window inched down slowly, as if unconvinced that removing the obstacle between them was wise.

He waited until she pulled the key back out of the ignition to speak. "I didn't mean to make you uncomfortable. You should go back in there and join Kelly. I'll leave if you want." His voice was deeper than usual.

She blinked. His eyes were darker than ever, like he could see directly into her thoughts. She shivered. The light must be playing tricks on her eyes. Or she needed something to eat.

He took a step back and held up his hands. "Look, I know I tried to kiss you last night, and I'm sorry. You have every right to report me for sexual harassment, and I won't try to stop you."

Ashley's mouth dropped open. She shook her head. "I didn't even think about reporting you. I just—well . . ." She cleared her throat and forced herself to keep eye contact. "I just changed my mind."

A look of relief passed over his face. "Well, you should come inside and eat." He tilted his head towards the house.

Ashley sighed. If she went inside, she'd have to remember who he really was—an arrogant doctor who could get any woman he wanted.

"I'll leave if I make you uncomfortable." He raised his hands, palms facing out in defeat.

She pinched the back of her hand. She needed to focus. He wasn't a good guy, no matter how much his eyes made her knees melt. "I really don't feel like being around anyone tonight. I'm just going to head home."

She gave him a wave and pressed the button to raise her car window, but the window didn't budge.

She groaned silently. Of course the window wouldn't move; she hadn't turned the key to activate the battery.

She tried again to raise the window. It raised a fraction of an inch, then stopped and wouldn't budge.

Michael stood there, watching.

"Everything ok?"

"My car is temperamental. She'll be fine, though." Ashley turned the key to start the engine, but nothing happened. She tried again. And again. She closed her eyes and held her breath, and tried again. Nothing.

She would not be the damsel in distress. She reached down and jabbed the button to release the car hood. Michael took a few steps back as she opened the car door and walked to the front of the vehicle, rain falling gently the whole time. She opened the hood and gazed thoughtfully. If she acted like she knew what she was looking at, then maybe he would walk away.

No luck. He stepped next to her.

"What do you think the problem is?" Michael asked her quietly.

She thought for a minute, keeping her eyes on the engine. "I got a new battery last month. The mechanic said something about the low level of coolant. Could be a problem with that or the oil or the fan belt or the internal combustors." She ticked the possibilities off her fingers.

He raised an eyebrow and scratched his chin. "Sounds reasonable."

The muscles surrounding her mouth twitched. She placed her hand over her mouth, but it didn't help. A chuckle escaped her lips.

He bent forward and touched something near the car battery. "What's so funny?"

"I think you know as much about cars as I do." She stopped trying to cover her laugh.

He stopped poking the engine. "I know enough about cars."

"You do? Go ahead, show off what you know." She stepped back and placed her hands on her hips.

He hesitated, then started laughing. "I have no idea what's

wrong with your car. I completely destroyed my chance to come to your rescue."

Her smile morphed into a gasp. "You want to come to my rescue?" No one had said anything like that to her since her parents died.

He stopped laughing and looked back at the car engine. "I'm sure you can take care of yourself. I just thought I might impress you if I took care of this for you. Give you a little help. But clearly, I spent too much time studying and not enough time learning basic mechanics." He spoke softly. "The best I can do is call a tow truck."

"Thank you?" She cleared her throat. "I mean, thanks. I don't need a tow truck, though. Kelly never minds keeping my car for a few days when it breaks down. At least I didn't block her in this time."

She closed the hood and walked back to the driver's seat. She turned the key a few more times, but the car refused to cooperate. She gripped the steering wheel and stuck her head out the open car door. "You can head inside. Tell Kelly I'll be there in a few minutes."

He stepped forward. "It's about to rain hard."

She closed her eyes for a second. A vision of kissing him in the rain popped into her imagination. She opened her eyes again quickly. "I know. I don't need much time. You can go inside without me."

He shook his head and placed his hand on top of the open car door. "What if a robber stopped by?"

She narrowed her eyes and tried not to laugh. "I'd let them take my car. They wouldn't get far in it." She turned back to the wheel and removed the keys from the ignition. "Seriously, you should go back inside. You aren't even wearing shoes." She bit her lip and looked through the car, out the passenger side window. The street lamp threw off a weak beam of light, and the clouds threatened to break into a downpour at any second. No one would be around to witness a robber or mugger sneak up on her. She shivered.

Michael let out a loud breath. He walked away without speaking.

Ashley leaned out the car door. She would not call him back. She could protect herself. She stepped out of the car, opened the trunk, and grabbed the roll of duct tape.

Footsteps approached from behind her, and she whirled around. Michael stood in front of her, holding a heavy jacket in his outstretched hand. "You look cold." His eyes darted from her eyes to her lips, where they lingered for a moment before moving back to her eyes. He stepped forward and wrapped the jacket around her shoulders. His scent immediately surrounded her.

She searched his eyes, and her stomach turned to knots. She bit her lip. He wasn't a regular guy. He was a doctor, the man who demanded attention when he roamed the hallways of the hospital. He drove a car that cost more than she made in a year. Two years. She shuddered. Maybe more than she even made in three years. She shouldn't feel anything for him. She had her own life, and he had his. They lived in two completely different worlds. And if she didn't act quickly, her world would include a broken car soaked with rainwater.

She sucked in a deep breath. "Kelly's recycle bin is in the garage. Can you find a large piece of cardboard?" She looked down.

His hand gently touched her chin, raising her face until her gaze met his again. "Do you need duct tape too?"

She lowered her gaze to his lips. "I have a roll here." She held up her hand between them. He placed his other hand on her shoulder and traced his fingers down the length of her arm until he reached her hand. Her skin tingled as he took the tape.

When he released her chin and walked over to the garage

door, she leaned against the side of the car and closed her eyes. She needed to get a handle on things before her imagination took over.

Michael returned with a thick piece of cardboard. He meticulously taped the cardboard to the open section of the car window, sealing it with layers of duct tape.

Her head started to spin, and her heart beat wildly. Not even a cold shower could save her now.

CHAPTER 20

Ashley bent over the steaming-hot bowl of soup sitting in front of her at Kelly's table while Michael laughed at something Kelly said. He still hadn't picked up his spoon. Kelly reached for a piece of bread from the basket in the center of the table and slowly spread butter on top. Michael touched the spoon, moved it an inched, and then released the spoon from his grasp and instead reached for the breadbasket.

Ashley sank in her chair. She should have made a salad to go along with the soup. Or something else, altogether. Anything except her family's most guarded recipe. Her mom didn't even share the recipe with the newspaper when the dish won first prize at the state fair twenty years ago.

Kelly said something else. Whatever she said must have been funny because Michael chuckled again while he spread butter on his bread. Ashley forced a smile on her face. She should have left when she had the chance. If she discovered that the car wouldn't work even minutes earlier, she could have walked to the bus stop before Michael had the chance to go outside and find her.

Finally, Michael stopped spreading butter on his bread

and reached for his spoon with his left hand. She'd never noticed he was left-handed. She twisted the corner of her lip. He wrote with his right hand at work. Maybe he used his left hand to eat and his right hand to write.

In slow motion, he dipped the spoon in the bowl, then raised it to his mouth. The spoon held a piece of dumpling and carrots. He opened his mouth, put the food in, and closed his mouth over it, then chewed slowly and swallowed.

Ashley stood up. "I'm going to check the food in the oven."

Kelly motioned for her to sit down. "I took it out of the oven already. Looked perfect."

Ashley sank into her chair again. She glanced at Michael out of the corner of her eye. He ate another spoonful of soup. "Kelly, what do you think of the food?" Maybe Michael would get the hint and say something too.

Kelly took a sip from her spoon. "It's exactly what I expected."

That was no help. Kelly usually raved about the soup. She turned to Michael and tried to look relaxed. "Is yours hot enough? I hope it didn't cool down too much while we were, um, outside."

He glanced up at her, spoon halfway to his mouth. He hesitated, then put the spoon back in the bowl. "Did you actually make this?"

She tilted her head. "Yes."

"From scratch?"

She nodded.

"In Kelly's kitchen, just now?"

"Well, yes and no. I made the broth the other day but made the rest of the dish tonight."

"Whose recipe did you use?"

She hesitated. "It's been in my family for decades, but . . ." The words caught in her throat. Her leg muscles twitched, and she tapped her foot on the floor. "My parents and I made some improvements to the recipe when I was a kid."

He took another sip of the soup and groaned in satisfaction. "Are your parents chefs or something?"

Ashley picked up her spoon and stirred her soup. She shook her head.

Kelly jumped in. "Ashley is one of the best cooks you'll ever meet. She has a natural knack for cooking."

Michael smiled. "It really is amazing soup."

Ashley sat up taller and stopped tapping her foot. He liked her soup. He even said it was amazing. The corners of her mouth turned up. She looked down at the soup to hide her expression. "It's nothing, really."

Michael looked at her after swallowing another bite. "You should consider opening up a restaurant or cafe. I bet you'd have people lined up around the corner."

She shook her head and felt her cheeks catch on fire. "I only cook for fun. I'll never do it for money."

"You could at least go to culinary school."

Ashley's stomach churned. She raised her gaze to Kelly and frowned. "Kelly, did you tell him—"

Kelly interrupted her and turned to Michael. "Ashley has different goals in life. She'd be the star student in any cooking class, but she's on her way to graduate school to become a social worker."

Ashley clenched her teeth. Kelly barely masked the disappointment in her voice.

"Really? Which school?"

Ashley sighed. "That's the problem." She looked at Kelly and tried to ignore Michael's presence. "I just heard back from the last school. I wasn't accepted, but they didn't reject me either. I'm on the waitlist."

Kelly smiled and reached forward, patting Ashley's hand with enthusiasm. "That's good! Better than nothing. There's still a chance, and if you don't get in this year, you can try again next year."

Michael had the good sense to eat the rest of his soup in silence.

A few more minutes went by before Kelly broke in again. "So Ashley, how was work today? Thanks again for covering my shifts."

"It was alright. Jessica says hello."

"She's so sweet. Did Gwen get on your case today?"

"No, she didn't, and actually, she was really weird. She stopped me before lunch and assigned me a brand new cleaning cart. She said something about someone complaining about the old cart. Can you believe it? I told her about the broken wheel almost every day, and she acted like she never knew about it until someone else complained. Did you say something to her?"

"No, I didn't say anything today, but it's about time. I never knew how you managed to drag around that broken cart day after day."

"Well, I could kiss whoever it was who complained to Gwen about that." Ashley glanced a look at Michael out of the corner of her eye. Should she ask him about his day? What was the normal thing to do when talking to a doctor outside of work? He looked odd, though. His cheeks were flushed and he scratched his neck. A thought hit her like a ton of bricks.

"Um, Michael, you aren't allergic to anything, are you? Your face looks really red." The newspaper would go crazy with a story like that: "Hospital Cleaner Kills Famous Doctor, Sentenced to Life in Prison"

He coughed and shook his head. "No, I'm fine. I'm not allergic to anything." She raised her eyebrows at him. "I promise, I'm just, um . . ." He snapped his fingers. "Can I have the soup recipe? I have a friend who owns a restaurant downtown. *Harvest House.* He might be interested in buying the recipe from you."

Ashley gasped. "You know Chef Houghton?"

He nodded. "Jeff and I go back a long time. I was the best man at his wedding. He told me the other day that he wants to change his menu again. He's coming up with new recipes."

"You think he'd actually like this soup?" She studied his face. Kelly liked her food, but she was family. Family was supposed to support one another. But Michael had no reason to lie.

"I can't make any guarantees, but this soup is pretty incredible. He pays top dollar for new recipes. Can I send him your recipe?"

Ashley's head started spinning. *Top dollar.* That sounded like enough for a deposit on an apartment and maybe a car repair. There might even be enough money to set aside for graduate school expenses.

She squeezed her eyes shut and shook her head. "No."

"No?" He stared at her as if she had two heads.

"I don't share this recipe with anyone. It's not for sale." She crossed her arms and stared at him—end of discussion.

He paused. "But wouldn't the money be helpful? I can't imagine that the hospital pays you very much, and your car needs work. Plus, grad school is expensive. Wouldn't extra money make things easier?"

She deepened her glare. There was no need for his pity. "I can take care of myself, and my financial situation is none of your business. Some things can't be bought. My recipe is one of them."

He opened his mouth, then closed it. He looked over to Kelly, who shrugged.

"Ashley won't even give this recipe to me."

He planted his gaze on Ashley again. "If not this recipe, you probably have others you could sell."

She stood up. "Done eating? There are brownies in the kitchen. I'll be back." She grabbed his half-eaten bowl of soup along with Kelly's empty bowl.

She walked out of the room and placed the bowls in the sink. She inhaled deeply and splashed cold water on her face. He didn't know. She couldn't blame him for not knowing. He had no idea that she dreamed of becoming a professional chef. To look around a restaurant and know that the customers were eating food she had made from recipes that she'd perfected. He also had no idea that her parents hated that plan. And he had no idea that they died the same day she argued with them about dropping out of college to attend culinary school instead.

He had no idea about any of that, and she acted like a fool by storming out of the room with the rest of his meal. He'd probably run away before she returned with the brownies. She strained her ears, but no sounds floated through from the dining room.

She splashed her face with water again. It didn't help. She shouldn't have let her imagination run wild and think she had a chance with him. He only helped her with her car because he was polite. No other reason. Even if he did like her, she ruined any chance she'd ever have.

She dried her hands on the kitchen towel and grabbed the brownies. She couldn't stay out of the dining room any longer unless she wanted both of them to think she forgot how to walk from one room to another.

Taking the brownies and a knife in one hand and a stack of small plates in the other, she straightened her spine and entered the dining room again. Michael and Kelly sat at the table, deep in whispered conversation.

Kelly glanced up, and her eyes widened at the sight of Ashley. She nudged Michael with her elbow, and he turned to her, ducking his head.

A ball formed in the pit of Ashley's stomach. There was no reason she should have been so rude to him. She shouldn't have taken away his food before he finished. Now, she bit her lip and cut the brownies, placing a large one on his plate and then setting it in front of him. "You aren't allergic to anything, are you? Nuts?"

He shook his head. "Looks good."

Kelly stole the plate and brownie from in front of him and pressed her lips together.

Ashley held her breath. She recognized Kelly's look. Michael needed to watch his step or he'd face her wrath. His insides had probably already turned to ice.

Michael reached out and grabbed the plate back from Kelly. Bold move.

Kelly picked up her forked and speared his brownie. She left the empty plate in front of him and held the brownie on the fork like a prized trophy.

Whatever those two were arguing about, Kelly won. Kelly walked out of the dining room with her brownie.

"What happened? Do you want another brownie?" Ashley lowered her voice to a whisper.

He shook his head. "Nothing. Yes. I mean, yes to the brownie."

She cut another generously sized brownie and placed it on a clean plate. She started to cut one for herself, then stopped. "I should really go home. It's getting late." She started to stand up from her chair.

"Wait." He reached out and placed his hand on her arm gently. He cleared his throat. "I'm sorry if I upset you when I asked for the soup recipe. I respect that it's a family secret. Some things can't be sold. But how about I introduce you to Jeff and his wife instead? I could arrange a meeting."

Ashley's jaw dropped. "You'd introduce me to Chef Houghton? That'd be amazing!"

He nodded.

"Absolutely!" She tried to control the smile spreading across her face. She cleared her throat and focused on speaking slowly, like a regular person and not a super-fan. "I mean, yes. That sounds nice."

"Tomorrow night good for you?"

"Yes!"

"Great. I'll pick you up at seven."

CHAPTER 21

Friday morning passed in a blur. Ashley's stomach protested loudly by the time she met Emily in the hospital cafeteria for lunch. She placed her lunch bag on the table and flopped down in the chair. "Sorry I'm late."

"Everything ok?" Emily glanced up from her half-eaten lunch.

"Just running behind schedule today. I spilled a big bottle of hand soap, and it exploded all over the floor. Anyway, I need your help." She reached for her lunch bag and opened it, withdrawing a container of pasta salad. "I have a thing tonight. Can I borrow something to wear?"

"What kind of thing?" Emily stabbed her salad with a fork and took a bite.

"I'll tell you if you promise not to freak out."

Emily put her fork on the cafeteria tray and crossed her arms. "I'm making no promises. But if you want to borrow something to wear, I need all the details."

Ashley laughed. "Fine. Michael and I are going to meet Chef Houghton at his restaurant tonight."

Emily's mouth dropped open. "Michael? Are you talking about Dr. Tobers? Same guy we ran into at the bar?"

Ashley nodded. "He came to Kelly's house last night when I was cooking. She never told me that she's known him since he was a kid. Anyway, he offered to introduce me to Chef Houghton. Can I borrow a dress?"

"He asked you out on a date?" She let out a squeal.

"Shh!" She glanced around, but no one looked interested in their conversation. "It's not a date, and the rest of the hospital does not need to know about this. It's just a business meeting."

"It is definitely not a business meeting."

Ashley rolled her eyes and took a bite of her sandwich.

"Did he say anything to you this morning?"

"I haven't seen him at all. I'm cleaning in the labor and delivery unit today."

"Are you meeting at the restaurant, or is he picking you up?"

"He's going to pick me up at my apartment."

Emily raised her eyebrows and smirked.

Ashley threw a clean napkin at Emily, which she batted away. "Don't look at me like that! It's not a date. He's only picking me up because my car broke down at Kelly's yesterday."

"How did you get home? Did he drive you home too? Did you kiss?"

"Shh! People are going to hear you. He didn't drive me home. I borrowed Kelly's car. I drove it to work today, but I need to drop it off at her house before the date. I mean, the meeting. Can you meet me there after work?"

"Sure. I'll run by my house, grab some dresses for you, and then meet you at Kelly's around five-thirty. What time is the date?"

"Seven. It's not a date."

"Fine." Emily glanced at her phone and groaned. "I have to run. I'll see you later." Emily picked up her tray and left the table.

Ashley stared at her pasta and took a small bite. It wasn't a date. They were going to go to a restaurant together, have a meeting with the chef, and discuss food. A business meeting. Michael wasn't interested in her like that. He probably only invited her to the meeting because Kelly encouraged him. That was it. Nothing romantic.

She caught movement out of the corner of her eye. Theresa, the nurse, sat at a nearby table, finishing her lunch while looking like she had stepped away from a modeling shoot for teal scrubs.

Ashley sighed. Michael sounded convincing when he told her that he wasn't interested in Theresa. But it would make much more sense for him to date Theresa instead of her. Theresa had a perfect life. She had a good job, she was beautiful, and she constantly bragged about going on vacations or weekend trips.

Not like her. The closest thing she'd had to a vacation in years was an afternoon flipping through a travel magazine that a patient left after getting discharged from the hospital.

Michael deserved to be with someone like Theresa. Someone who wasn't broken.

Ashley's hands shook as she reached for the empty pasta container and her lunch bag. She shoved the container in the bag and fumbled with the zipper. Someone placed a manicured hand with bright pink nails on the chair that Emily had vacated and pulled it away from the table. Ashley glanced up as Theresa sat down.

"I heard you talking a few minutes ago."

Ashley faced Theresa. It wasn't like Theresa could have heard her thoughts. "What do you mean?"

"I heard you talking about going on a date with Dr.

Tobers. Why would he be interested in you?" Her eyes narrowed as she looked over Ashley.

"Oh." Ashley glanced down at the table in front of her as heat rose in her cheeks.

"I'm going to be nice and give you a warning. You don't want to go after someone like him. You'll never get him, and you'll just hurt yourself in the process."

Ashley swallowed hard. She glanced around to see if anyone at the nearest table could overhear them. Hopefully, the noise of the cafeteria would drown out Theresa's voice. However, if Theresa overheard Emily, then anyone nearby could probably hear Theresa. Her throat tightened.

"He's too far out of your league, so don't get your hopes up. Even if he were to go on a date with you, it would be a pity date. You'll never interest him for long. Once he gets what he wants, he'll move on to someone better. Like me." Theresa rapped her manicured nails on the tabletop and continued talking in her high-pitched voice. "But go ahead on the date tonight. Enjoy the water, because we both know that's the only item on the menu that you'll be able to afford. Unless you actually think he'd pay for your meal without expecting something else in return."

Ashley's mouth dropped open. She hadn't thought about that. Theresa was right. How was she ever going to pay for her food at a fancy restaurant? She still needed to wait for her next paycheck to buy milk. Her bank account would cry at the sight of the cheapest item on the menu.

Theresa stood up and delicately released a used napkin from her hand. "Oops, I dropped some garbage. You can clean it up for me." She leaned in close and lowered her voice. "Don't forget. This is your warning. He's mine, so stay away." She straightened up again and walked away.

Ashley watched her leave, numb and not sure what to think. She glanced around again, but no one noticed her. At least there were no obvious witnesses to what just happened. She leaned over, picked the napkin up from the ground, and placed it next to her lunch sack. It was crumpled, dirty, and useless, just like her.

Theresa was right. She didn't belong with someone like Michael.

CHAPTER 22

Ashley's doorbell buzzed promptly at 7 p.m. Ashley froze in front of the bathroom mirror, mascara wand hovering millimeters from her eyelashes, and looked at Emily's reflection.

"I told you he'd show up for the date." Emily's smug expression pulled Ashley out of her thoughts.

She stuck her tongue out at Emily. Immature, but completely appropriate.

Emily rolled her eyes in return. "I'm going to let him in. I'll give you five minutes to finish getting ready. After that, I'm bringing out your baby pictures and telling him all about the time you were two years old, stripped naked and —"

"Emily!" Ashley dropped the mascara wand and gave her cousin a shove.

"You've been warned. Hurry." With one last glance, Emily left to let in Ashley's date.

Butterflies took up residency in her stomach. He actually showed up. Unless it was just a coincidence and the person at her apartment door was delivering a package? Her front door creaked in protest as it opened and Emily's voice, louder than usual, greeted the visitor. Michael was here.

Here, inside her apartment. She knew the moment was coming, but her stomach twisted. She should have met him at the restaurant. She should have borrowed a car or walked there instead of letting him inside her place. He probably had nice, designer furniture. Even his office had better furniture than her apartment. Her old orange couch belonged in a 1980's house of horror, and her mismatched end tables were no better. She found them on the curb, waiting for the garbage truck one morning as she drove to work. The coat of white paint didn't make them look rustic or shabby chic, as promised by the blogger who posted hundreds of furniture makeovers. But they did look better than her coffee table, which was another curb-side rescue and made of laminate. The blogger didn't give any warnings about painting laminate furniture. Maybe she needed to drive through the wealthier side of town on garbage day.

She frowned at her reflection. As Emily had not-so-gently reminded her barely an hour ago when she showed up with a dress for Ashley to wear, he was interested in her and not what she owned. There was no reason to be embarrassed about her apartment. It was clean and comfortable.

She took a deep breath and checked the time on her phone. Somehow, three minutes had already sped by. She gave her hair one last pat, finished putting on her mascara, and then stared at her reflection in the full-length mirror. Emily's dress was amazing. Dark purple, tight in all the right spots, and showed a decent amount of leg. Much better than the old, faded dress in her closet. She looked like she might even belong in a restaurant with Michael.

Except her earrings. She touched the earring dangling from her right earlobe. They weren't right. She rushed into her bedroom closet. What had she and Emily been thinking when Emily pulled out that set of earrings and gushed over how perfect they would be? They were too shiny, too large, and—

Her thoughts were interrupted by a loud voice in the next room. "So Michael, did you know that Ashley and I are cousins? I know everything about her, even where she keeps her photo albums. Give me a minute and I'll show you some pictures of her while we wait."

No, no, no. Ashley flung open the flimsy door separating her bedroom and living room. Emily had her hand on a photo album, and Michael sat on the other end of the couch. He stared at her as she stepped into the room. He slowly stood up, glancing up and down her body.

Ashley stood, speechless. Did he just check her out? Chills spread over her body. She bit her lip to stop the giddy smile that threatened to take over her face.

Emily frowned. "Ashley, I was just about to show him your baby photos!"

Ashley walked over to her, grabbed the album, and dropped it on the end table. "Another time, I guess." She paused, feeling awkward. "Um, Michael, you know Emily."

"I do. Thanks again for your help at work today, Emily."

"Anytime." Emily stood and picked up her jacket. "I'm leaving. You two have fun tonight. Don't do anything I wouldn't do." She waved her fingers at Michael, then pulled Ashley in tight for a hug. She whispered quietly enough that only Ashley could hear. "Relax and have fun. You deserve it. He's a lucky man to have you for a date."

"It's a meeting," she whispered back.

Emily released her and left, closing the door behind her.

The living room felt smaller than ever.

She looked at Michael, only to see that he'd picked up something while her attention had been on Emily. Flowers.

He held them out to her and cleared his throat. "You look amazing. I've been looking forward to this all day."

"Thanks." Ashley's face grew warm. The bouquet was a beautiful arrangement of daisies, her favorite. She took them from his hands and lifted them to her nose, taking a deep inhale. No man had ever given her flowers before. "I'll go put these in water, and then I'll be ready to go."

She walked across the living room in five steps and stood in front of the kitchen sink. She didn't own a vase. There was no need for a vase when she had no money to buy flowers and had no one to buy flowers for her. There must be something she could put her flowers in, though. An old milk bottle? No, the opening would be too small. Maybe one of her saucepans? That wouldn't work either. She glanced at the corner of her kitchen, where she kept her recycling bin. A glass bottle that had previously contained peanut butter lay in the otherwise empty bin, but the jar was too small for this bouquet. She opened and closed one cabinet door, then turned to the other cabinet. Her child-hood cookie jar sat on the top shelf, above the mismatched plates. It would be the perfect size. Except she couldn't reach it.

"Michael, can you come here and give me a hand?" She offered him a smile. He hadn't run away last night when her car broke, and he hadn't run away at the sight of her apart-ment. Maybe this wouldn't be too bad.

He glanced around the room as he walked up next to her and held up his hand. "My hand is yours. Where do you want it?"

"What?" She replayed his words in her head.

"You asked me to come in and give you a hand. Here's the hand." He chuckled at his own joke.

"I, um . . . well, I don't have a vase, so I was going to grab an old cookie jar, but it's too high for me to reach." She pointed to the cabinet next to her. "Can you get it? Top shelf." She held her breath.

He turned and placed his hand on her waist while easily reaching up with his other hand to bring down the cookie jar. Then he moved his hand away from her waist and turned on the faucet. A stream of water gurgled out, and he carefully filled the jar, like people in his world regularly filled their mansions with flowers placed in cookie jars.

Some water sloshed onto the counter as he turned off the water.

"Be careful, it's special." She reached out to steady the jar on the counter. Her hand touched his, and it might have been her imagination, but it almost looked like he moved his hand over hers on purpose.

"Looks old. Was it yours when you were a kid?" He picked up the flowers from the counter and removed the wrapping around the bouquet.

"Yes. My mom used to keep it full of cookies for my friends and me."

"What's your favorite kind of cookie?" Michael's voice was calm, comforting. No wonder his patients fawned over him.

The memory of mint teased her tongue. "When I was a kid, I loved these special chocolate peppermint cookies my mom made. She always let me add the chocolate chips to the batter and pretended not to see me eat half the bag. I still can't make those cookies without thinking of her."

"Sounds delicious. Do you still make them when you get together with her?" He placed the bouquet in the water, then turned to her with a satisfied grin on his face.

She frowned and grabbed a towel to wipe a drop of water on the counter. "We haven't made them together in a long time. Things are, well . . . different now." She looked at him again. She didn't want to lie. Not to him. She leaned over the flowers and took a deep breath. "She and my dad died a few years ago. Car accident."

"I'm sorry."

She looked back at him. He hovered above her, tall and strong. Those words didn't sound empty when he said them. "It's ok. It happened a few years ago, and, well . . ." she trailed off and shook her head. She needed to change the subject. "You know my favorite cookie. What's yours?"

He hesitated for a second before opening his mouth. "Promise you won't make fun of me?"

She laughed. "Make fun of what?"

"My favorite cookie is oatmeal raisin."

She shook her finger at him. "You're teasing me."

He shook his head. "I love oatmeal raisin cookies."

"That's the kind of cookie that grandmas make kids to give them something that sounds healthy. No one under the age of eighty could possibly say that's their favorite cookie."

He shrugged. "It's my favorite. What can I say?" He flashed her a grin.

"Well, it's only your favorite because you haven't had any cookies that I baked."

"I have had your cookies. I still love oatmeal raisin."

She gasped. "Liar."

"Nope." He stepped closer to her and put his hands on her shoulders. He leaned his head in close and said, in almost a whisper, "Kelly sneaks me some of the treats you bring in to work. I've had your cookies, your brownies, your cake, everything. I still love oatmeal raisin."

She placed her hand on his chest and gave him a slight push. He didn't move an inch. "I don't think I can go on a date with someone who loves oatmeal raisin cookies." She tried to keep a straight face while talking.

"Fine. I'll give you one more chance to convince me that there's a cookie out there that's better than oatmeal raisin."

"If you have any good taste at all, it won't be hard to do that."

"When will you make them for me?"

She thought for a second. "Tomorrow afternoon. I'll bring them to work on Monday."

"Won't they taste better fresh out of the oven?"

"Absolutely, but—"

He interrupted her. "Then I'll be here tomorrow afternoon, and we'll make them together. One o'clock work for you?"

She looked at his eyes closely. He looked serious. "Ok . . ."

"Ok?" He raised his eyebrows.

"Let's make cookies tomorrow." Was this actually happening? She had to call Emily and tell her all about it. He wanted to see her again, and their date hadn't even started. Well, business meeting. But he wouldn't bring flowers for a business meeting or look at her like that if this wasn't a date. She definitely needed to call Emily and tell her about their plans to make cookies. Unless making cookies was code for something else . . . a chill ran through her.

"Look, Michael . . ." She lowered her gaze from his eyes before she got lost in their depths and forgot what she was going to say. "Thanks again for arranging this meeting with Chef Houghton. But I think we should cancel." She should never have agreed to date him. He was out of her league. Theresa knew it. She knew it. And she needed to focus on graduate school. To make her parents proud by becoming a social worker, not spending her time dating.

"Does this have anything to do with what Theresa said to you in the cafeteria today?" His voice came out strained.

She shrugged. "Yes. No." She shook her head. "It's more than that. But how did you know—"

"Theresa was wrong. Her opinion doesn't matter. It's just you and me tonight."

Ashley shook her head. "I'm sorry to disappoint you."

"Ashley." He placed his hand under her chin and gently raised it so that her eyes were staring straight into his. "Say it one more time, and we'll cancel tonight. I hope you don't, but I'll respect your choice. We can go on this date, or go as friends, and I'll introduce you to Chef Jeff. Nothing more than that."

Ashley considered his words. He sounded convincing, and she believed him when he said he'd leave if she wanted to cancel the date. But, her heart sank at the thought of turning her back on him. She didn't want to cancel. Not really. She wanted to be close to him. Her legs had never felt like they'd give out from just one look before. She swallowed and nodded her head.

He let go of her chin and clasped her hand, then turned, pulling her gently. "Let's leave before the restaurant closes."

CHAPTER 23

Ashley's stomach flip-flopped when Michael pulled the car into the restaurant parking lot. She'd worried about the car ride to the restaurant all day. Would they run out of things to talk about? Would she be able to speak like an actual human being and make sense while she spoke? She shouldn't have worried about that at all. The short car ride ended before she had time to get nervous. But now that they pulled into the parking lot, her stomach somersaulted over and over.

Michael kept a firm grip on Ashley's hand as they walked up to the maître d'. She leaned over to his ear and whispered. "Do you think there's any chance we can sit near the kitchen? It would be amazing to catch a glimpse of them working back there, or maybe even get a glimpse of the chef."

Michael squeezed her hand and winked. "Leave it to me."

The maître d' greeted them, and Michael leaned forward to talk quietly. The woman gave them a brief look of surprise before glancing at the computer screen in front of her. Ashley looked around the entrance to the restaurant. The building looked like it used to be an old Victorian mansion, with incredibly high ceilings, rustic wooden floors, and lush plants lining the dimmed entry. Quiet music set a romantic, hushed tone. She stood on her tiptoes and peered around the hostess, who still tapped buttons on the computer screen. Behind her, almost out of sight, was the back of a small grand piano. A woman in a glimmering dress sat in front of the piano, playing the music. Ashley inhaled deeply. The restaurant dripped with glamour. It was exactly the type of restaurant she had dreamed of cooking in as a child.

The maître d' motioned for them to follow her. She led them through the restaurant to the large wooden doors separating the dining area from the kitchen. Michael tightened his grip on Ashley's hand and only smiled in response to the confused look she gave him.

The maître d' opened the door to the kitchen and motioned for them to follow. As they walked, she spoke over her shoulder. "The kitchen area is normally reserved for only kitchen staff. Tonight, you'll be allowed here as long as you follow certain rules. Only walk where I walk. I will seat you at your table. Once seated, please do not get up. If you need anything at all, your server will be waiting nearby to help you."

The noise and organized chaos within the brightly lit kitchen were overwhelming. People hustled from counter to counter, knives made sharp cuts on vegetables, and countless pots and pans sizzled on multiple stovetops. Every few seconds, someone yelled "Hot plate!" as they moved skillets and pans.

In the midst of the chaos, Ashley thought the hostess actually said that they'd be in the kitchen for the evening. She shook her head and tried to focus on where they were walking.

A few feet in front of them, a small table was set with two place settings. It was tucked into a corner of the large kitchen, far enough to the side that they wouldn't be in the way, yet positioned so that Ashley had a great view of the staff working at the stoves, ovens, and prep spaces.

This was already the best date that Ashley had ever been on. Michael must have been a mind reader or something. Maybe a magician. Unless this was all a dream? She used her free hand to pinch her arm. It hurt. She wasn't dreaming.

Michael released her hand when they approached the table and pulled out a chair for her. She sat, then waited until he was seated before asking the question that had been on the tip of her tongue since they entered the large room.

"How did you get us back here? Is this really happening? What did—?"

She was interrupted by a loud booming voice. "Michael! You finally made it!"

Ashley looked in the direction of the voice to see a tall man with flaming red hair walking towards them. He carried a bottle of wine.

"Jeff, good to see you." Michael stood up and embraced the man briefly. Casually. As if it was a normal thing to have a walking legend of culinary arts greet you in the kitchen of his restaurant.

Ashley couldn't feel her legs—or the rest of her body. She stared.

Jeff turned to Ashley. "You must be Ashley. I heard a lot about you." Jeff stepped over and gave Ashley a hug. She tried to hug him back without resorting to twelve-year-old behavior by jumping and screaming at decibels that could cause hearing loss. "Brought you some wine. Thought it would pair well with the first course." He held up the bottle in his hand.

Michael took one glance at Ashley and then turned back to his friend, who already poured one glass of wine. "How's your wife doing?" He spoke like they were hanging out at a coffee shop instead of the kitchen of the best restaurant in the city.

Jeff let out a deep laugh and poured a second glass of wine. "She's great. Out of town this week, visiting her sister. She's furious that she's not here tonight to see you and meet Ashley." He handed the glass of wine to Ashley. "I've been trying to get Michael to bring a date here for years, but you are the first."

Ashley paused, mouth open, and looked at Michael. He must have dated other women in the past. Why wouldn't he have brought past dates here? It didn't make sense. He could get a table at the best restaurant in the city at a moment's notice. Why wouldn't he bring every date here?

Ashley watched Jeff and Michael chat for a few more minutes before Jeff returned to the stove. Once alone again, Ashley picked up the cloth napkin and smoothed it over her lap. Somehow, the noise and organized chaos of the kitchen comforted her, giving her strength and relaxing her nerves. She cleared her throat.

"Was Jeff really telling the truth? I'm the first date you've brought here?"

Michael shrugged his shoulders and gave her a crooked grin. "True. I haven't actually been here in over a year. Not the kind of place that Bill and I hang out at after work."

She laughed as his words sunk in. "So I'm really the first date you've brought here?"

"Yes."

"Hmm." She liked the thought of that. She waited as one of the line cooks brought a plate of food to their table. Jeff shouted something indecipherable across the kitchen to them. The cook briefly described the dish as he placed it on the table, but Ashley didn't pay attention. She was more interested in her date across the table.

Michael watched the cook as he spoke, nodding his head

slowly. He ran his hand over his jawline, brow furrowed and head tilted slightly. That look tugged at her memory. Unless she was mistaken, he had a similar expression on his face the other night when he'd tried to diagnose her car problems.

The cook left, and Michael picked up his fork. He hesitated, fork hovering above the plate. He barely resembled the serious, focused man from the hospital.

She took her glass of wine and sipped it, then tasted the appetizer in front of her. There was an assortment of mushrooms with orzo arranged artfully on the plate with a small piece of parsley to the side. She closed her eyes and focused on the flavors in the sauce. There was a salty taste, possibly from parmesan cheese. The earthy mushroom flavor was just right. Not overpowering, but enough to satisfy her taste buds. She needed to commit this taste to memory so that she could try to recreate it after the next payday.

She opened her eyes and saw Michael staring at her intently. His fork still hovered over his untouched plate.

"I have never seen someone so excited about the food they ate."

Ashley took another sip of wine. The wine tasted more earthy and full after the bite of food. She loved how food and wine influenced each other. "Anyone with taste buds would be excited about this food."

"I guess so." He leaned back in his chair, studying her curiously. "I never understood food. Jeff used to try out his new dishes on me back in college when we shared an apartment with a few other guys. There were some nights when he made three or four versions of the same dish, and he'd get so mad when I couldn't taste any difference between them or tell him which one tasted the best. He finally took over cooking for the entire house after I burnt the food too many times."

She tried to picture him in a college apartment and failed. "You really can't cook?"

"I've given up on it. I usually eat take-out now. Have you always loved cooking?"

Ashley paused and thought over his question. "I guess you could say that. I started watching cooking shows with my mom when I was young, maybe four or five years old. We always made cookies and cakes on the weekends. By the time I turned ten, she let me make dinner a few nights each week. I was a little over-ambitious at first and made some really weird-tasting dishes. But it's now just second nature to me. I could spend all day cooking if I had the time."

"So why don't you become a chef?" Michael looked at her intently.

Ashley sighed. She'd walked right into dangerous territory. She decided to stick with the story that she told everyone else. It was mostly true.

"I'm going to be a social worker. It's a better job. Becoming a chef would take a long time, and it's not a real job." Ashley realized how shallow her words sounded as she spoke. "I mean, some people do really well as a chef, obviously." She tilted her head towards the stoves where Jeff and his kitchen staff worked in finely choreographed movements. "But it's not as stable a career as being a social worker. Remember how I told you that my parents died? I support myself. And hospitals always need more social workers. I won't have to worry about finding a job."

"If there's anything I've learned by being a doctor, it's that there are no guarantees of anything in life."

She sighed. He didn't take her excuses as easily as most people. "Yes, but being a chef is more of a dream. I have to be realistic. There's no one to help me if I fail. I don't come from money." Not to mention the debt that she'd inherited from her parents' funeral expenses.

Michael sighed and leaned back in his chair. Ashley could feel his eyes roaming over her as she stared down at her plate, unable to meet his eyes.

"Do you think I came from a wealthy family?"

Ashley glanced at him in his expensive suit. "Probably. You must have had to pay for college and medical school along the way. I have massive student loans from college."

"I was lucky. I had scholarships and took out a small loan to cover the rest. I didn't have family to rely on for money either." She raised her eyebrows at this confession. "Did Kelly tell you how we know each other so well? Why I spent so much time at her place?"

"No, she said it was your story to tell." She'd tried, though. She even bribed Kelly with the offer of making creme brûlée, Kelly's favorite. Kelly barely even winced as she rejected her.

"Sounds like something Kelly would say." He paused to take a drink of water before reaching across the table to hold her hand. He rubbed his thumb lightly over her knuckles as he continued talking. "My parents worked long hours, so Kelly watched me after school. She had a son, about five years younger than me. He ended up being like a little brother. When he was three years old, he needed surgery to fix a heart condition that he was born with. It was a risky surgery, and he didn't make it. I was devastated. Kelly and her husband were devastated too." He paused and took a deep breath before speaking again. She bit her lip. Kelly had mentioned her son many times. The story always gripped her heart even though she'd never met him. "I decided that I was going to be a doctor, a cardiologist. I was going to be better than the other doctors, better than the ones who couldn't save Bobby. Since then, I never looked back. I worked all through college and medical school to pay off the bills. I lived in a two-bedroom apartment with five other guys so we could afford rent. Walked to campus most days because my car was worse off than yours." He grinned at her. "And your car is pretty bad."

"Hey, don't make fun of my car! It's seen better days, but . . ." She laughed at the expression on his face. "Ok, it's a horrible car. I can't believe that your car could have been worse."

"A raccoon broke into my car once and made a mess. It took a month to get rid of all the smells."

"Ew, gross, you win!"

Ashley paused for a moment as she thought over what Michael had told her. She had no idea that he had struggled so much in the past. Putting himself through medical school, making sacrifices along the way to make his dream career come true. Maybe she'd judged him too quickly.

Her thoughts wandered back to something else he mentioned.

"I knew Kelly had a son who died at a young age. She told me about him a few times, and I saw his baby pictures in her house. I didn't know that you were close to him."

"Bobby was like my brother. He always followed me around and tried to do what I did. I remember it was annoying sometimes. Most of the time, however, I liked having him as a little shadow. He made me feel important. I promised to teach him how to make a basket in one of those little toddler basketball hoops after he recovered from open-heart surgery. He didn't make it off the table alive." Michael paused and took a deep breath. "I still think of him when I'm having a hard time or faced with a difficult case. His story still inspires me to do better. To live life more fully, which is something I have forgotten in the past few months. I've gotten too wrapped up in work and have forgotten to really live life." He gave Ashley's hand a firm squeeze. "That changes now. I've wasted so much time just focused on studying and being a better doctor that I haven't had the time to date in years. But there's something about you. I can't say exactly what it is, but I can't stop thinking about you. I'm not going to let you slip away from me."

Ashley's smile widened as he spoke. She must have looked like a high schooler being asked on a date. No man had ever been that direct with her about his feelings. She waited for the familiar knots in her stomach to form under his intense gaze, but there was something about his presence that comforted her. She wanted nothing more than to stare into his eyes for hours. Ugh. That sounded like something from a romance movie. She needed to get control of her brain again before she lost herself.

Fortunately, Jeff and an assistant approached their table with a large tray of dishes. They placed each small dish on the table, offering a sampling of the menu. Ashley's mouth hung open as she took in all the items in front of her. This was the height of culinary creations. A mecca for food. A table full of perfection, waiting to be savored.

She glanced at Jeff, who had pulled up a seat to the table and sat down comfortably. His assistant had already returned to the counter. Jeff, however, looked like he had nowhere else to be than at their table.

Jeff turned to Ashley. He selected a small plate from the center of the table and placed it in front of her. "I like to play a little guessing game with anyone who sits in the kitchen. Try this, and then tell me what's in it." He wiggled his eyebrows, clearly enjoying himself.

"How many ingredients are in it?" She studied the food on the plate. Several scallops were arranged in a circle over a creamy sauce, with strips of a pale vegetable placed on top. Several small green sprouts and little red seeds added a splash of color to the dish.

"About ten."

"How many ingredients do most people guess correctly?"

"Three, sometimes four. Most people recognize the scallops."

She bent over the plate and took a deep inhale. It smelled heavenly. She chose carefully for her first taste. She took a bite of scallop with the sauce. The scallop was the perfect texture, with a slightly salty taste.

She looked at Michael. "Do you want to guess the ingredients first, or should I?" He hadn't touched his fork yet.

He shook his head. "Go ahead. I would only embarrass myself."

Ashley took another bite, considering the tastes and texture carefully. "There's obviously scallop, and it tastes like it was lightly salted and then caramelized. The green bits on top are sprouts. I'd bet that they are watercress sprouts, but they could also be arugula sprouts." She paused and took a bit of the crunchy pale brown vegetable on top. "These are definitely fried parsnips that were deep-fried in canola oil, not air-fried or baked in the oven."

She tasted the cream sauce that was under the scallop she'd eaten. This sauce was a bit more complicated. She took another taste, letting the flavor fill her mouth. "This tastes like a puree of the parsnip with cream and some spices. I can taste curry, cumin, and turmeric. I might be missing something here, though." She took another taste before shrugging her shoulders. She couldn't identify the last flavor in the sauce, but she hardly cared. No one could care about anything after tasting a few bites of this dish.

She moved on to the last component of the dish: the small red seeds and the drizzle of red sauce at the plate's edges. "The red seeds are pomegranate, and it tastes like you made a simple pomegranate dressing from the juice."

Ashley looked up from her plate. Both Michael and Jeff stared at her. Her smile quickly faded away, replaced by a warm blush. She used to guess most of the ingredients when she played this game with her parents, but that had been years ago. Judging by their stares, she must have lost her talent for the game.

She looked back at her plate to escape the stares from both men and fidgeted with the cloth napkin on her lap.

Jeff spoke first. "Impressive. You only missed one ingredient. The puree also had coriander. You were right about the sprouts. They were watercress." Jeff shook his head at Ashley. "Very few people guessed as many ingredients as you did."

Michael joined in. "That was impressive."

Ashley's heart stammered from the praise. Playing this game with her mom was one thing, but doing it for a Michelin-rated chef was another. Not to mention that Michael stared at her as if he never wanted to look away.

Jeff picked another dish and placed it in front of her, offering the same challenge. Again, Ashley identified nearly every ingredient. He did the same with two more dishes, shaking his head in disbelief after each one. Finally, Michael spoke up.

"Jeff, are you still looking for another cook?"

Ashley looked up from the plate of food she was studying.

Jeff nodded. "Haven't found anyone up to the task yet."

"Ashley can cook."

Ashley looked back down at the plate of food in front of her. She lifted a small forkful to her mouth and chewed carefully before risking a glance back up.

Jeff leaned back in his chair. "I bet she can. No one could guess as many ingredients in these dishes if they didn't do a lot of cooking on their own." He turned to her. "You looking for a job?"

She shook her head. "I have a job, and I'm trying to go to graduate school. Social work." She looked back at Michael, expecting a look of disapproval. Instead, he nodded encouragingly.

"Jeff, she brings food to work all the time for her coworkers. Everything is amazing."

"I really don't think I should waste your time, Chef. I would love to work somewhere like here, but I can't." Her chest tightened. A job cleaning dishes in a restaurant like this would be amazing. Actually cooking here would be more than she could ever imagine. But it would also mean crushing her parents' dreams for her. She swallowed hard.

"Well, I have an opening, and you've earned an interview. You'd need to come in one morning and cook a few dishes with me here in the restaurant."

"Thanks, I'm flattered by the opportunity, but I'm really not interested." She tried to sound strong when she said the words, but her voice shook.

Jeff shrugged. She didn't even want to look at Michael to see his reaction, but she could feel the heat from his stare. She reached for her water and took a sip.

After a moment of silence, Michael cleared his throat and started to speak. "Ash—"

"Where's the ladies' room?" Ashley stood up as she spoke.

Jeff waved for the attention of one of the dishwashers. The woman dried her hands and walked over.

"Bathroom?" Ashley tried not to run out the door as she waited.

The dishwasher smiled at her, not aware of the stabbing pain in Ashley's heart caused by turning down a once-in-a-lifetime opportunity. A dream that she'd held since she was a child. A dream that could never come true. If she'd been brave, she'd have told Michael the truth. That her last conversation with her parents was an argument. She had wanted to drop out of college and go to culinary school. They wanted her to finish her last semester and earn her undergraduate degree in social work. She could never go back and erase their argument. She could never go back and make amends. The only way forward was to fulfill their wish. Become a social worker. Her dreams of becoming a chef had shattered the night her parents died.

The dishwasher turned and led Ashley away from the kitchen.

CHAPTER 24

Ashley returned to the table a few minutes later. Jeff was back to work, moving quickly around the kitchen. The third chair had been removed from the table, leaving the empty chair that was placed close to Michael's so that they could both view the bustling kitchen easily. But she couldn't just watch the kitchen staff all night. She still had to face Michael. Hopefully, it wouldn't be too awkward.

She sat down carefully at the table and watched his face. He looked normal. He didn't look at all concerned that she had nearly run away from the table moments before. Maybe this date wouldn't end in a disaster after all. She cleared her throat. "About what just happened, I didn't mean to—"

Michael cut her off. "I'm having a great time on this date. Between you and me—" he leaned in closer and lowered his voice to a whisper "—I haven't seen anyone turn Jeff down like that for a long time and the look on his face was price-less." He gave her a satisfied grin and reached his hand across the table.

She placed her hand in his. Just like before, it felt perfect. She leaned in a little closer. "You aren't upset?"

The corner of his mouth turned up slightly. "I am anything but upset. You have no idea how crazy you make me. Just when I think I have figured you out, you throw me a curveball."

"When have I ever thrown you a curveball?" She narrowed her eyes at him, almost gathering enough courage to tease him. It would definitely be easier if she could forget —even for just a few minutes—that he was the doctor she saw in the hospital hallways.

He paused and then started speaking slowly. "How about the time you messed up all my heart models in my office? Or when you stayed late a few weeks ago because one of my patients was alone and scared about their surgery the next day? Or how you were able to push around that rackety cleaning cart, day after day, and not collapse with exhaustion each night?" He placed his free hand on top of hers so that he was cupping her hand in both of his. He looked at their hands and started making little circles on the top of her hand with his finger. "My back and feet ached like crazy after just two hours of cleaning—" He cut himself off without finishing the sentence.

Ashley tilted her head. Her brain might be turning to mush from the feel of his hands wrapped around hers, but she wasn't that far gone yet. "What did you say?"

"Nothing. You just continue to surprise me. That's all." He resumed tracing circles on her hand.

She narrowed her eyes. "You said that your back and feet ached after two hours of cleaning." She paused, not sure if she should say what she was thinking or not. She studied Michael's face. He looked sheepish, like he was afraid that he was going to get in trouble for something. He was hiding something. She took a sip of wine with her free hand as she tried to determine her next step.

Maybe it was the wine, or maybe she was actually starting

to feel more comfortable around him, but something stirred in her. She took a deep breath. "You might be surprised to hear this, but the strangest thing happened to me at work last week. Right after we, um, well, right after I messed with your heart models and left your office, I accidentally fell asleep." She glanced at his face but couldn't read him. He was staring intently at their hands.

She took another sip of wine. "I must have been more tired than I thought because I don't even remember cleaning half of the offices in that section. But when I woke up, the offices were clean."

"Hmm." He slowly raised her hand and started massaging it.

She almost groaned out loud. It felt so good.

His voice was deeper when he spoke again. "You have beautiful hands."

She closed her eyes briefly. He kept massaging her hand, running his fingers over her palm and sending shivers up her spine.

He lifted her hand to his mouth and placed a kiss in her palm. This time, she couldn't stop the groan from escaping her lips. He spoke again, his voice starting to get gravelly. "Your hands are so soft."

She glanced at his face as the words sunk in. Something was wrong. She frowned, but her brain was barely working. She didn't really want to think about what he said. She just wanted him to kiss her hand again. And then kiss—

"Wait a minute." She pulled her hand out of his grasp and crossed her arms protectively. She glared at him. "My hands are not soft at all. They are always dry from the cleaning solutions at work, and I have calluses from cooking so much." She gasped with realization. "You're trying to distract me!"

At least he had the decency to look embarrassed. "Was it working?"

"Yes. No. Just tell me the truth."

"Fine." He shrugged and lifted his wine glass. Right as he placed the glass to his lips, he smiled, muttered quietly, and then took a sip.

"What did you say?" All her anxious energy from before had transformed at some point, and now she was just excited. And feeling bold. Between the wine, her amped-up emotions, and the way he was squirming uncomfortably in his seat, it was hard to imagine him as someone who could intimidate even a flea. She made her best attempt at making a serious face at him. He was hiding something, and she was going to find out what.

"You really want to know? Won't that ruin some of the mystery of our relationship?" He was actually joking with her now.

Two could play at this game. She frowned. "If you don't tell me, I will tell Jeff that you haven't been behaving and that you can't have dessert."

"I want my dessert." His voice had that gravelly edge again.

She shuddered. "Then tell me."

He shifted in his chair and picked up her hand again. "Fine. You looked so peaceful the other night when you were asleep on Dr. Jenner's couch. I couldn't imagine waking you up. Plus, I wanted to do something nice. I really messed up when I saw you at the bar and when I was pretending that I wasn't interested in you at work. I thought you'd only be angry if you found out that I helped you, especially after I tried to . . ." He shrugged.

She knew what he wasn't saying. The kiss. The night they almost kissed, and she turned away at the last moment. The kiss that could have been. The kiss that never was.

The kiss that she couldn't stop thinking about now. What would it feel like to kiss him? He was so confident and demanding at work. Would he be as demanding with his kiss? Or would he be gentle and slow, the way he'd been with her that night? More concerned about her enjoyment than his own?

She realized she was holding her breath and exhaled. When had her chair moved so close to Michael's? Had he shifted his seat when she wasn't watching? They were nearly seated next to each other on the side of the small round table. Close enough that she could feel the heat radiating off his body.

She reached for her wine to take another sip but hesitated. She moved her hand over a few inches and picked up her water glass instead. She took a sip of the cold water, but it did nothing to ease her thirst. She set it down again and tilted her head towards Michael.

What were they talking about? Kissing? No, that wasn't it. He had just told her something important. She leaned in closer to him, nearly whispering as she spoke. "So you did that for me? Cleaned while I slept?"

He didn't say anything, but he gave her the smallest of nods. "I'd do it again if you asked."

This was the moment. The words were on her lips, but she didn't know if she could actually say them. What if he said no? Or if she embarrassed herself? But he was the one who said that he wanted tonight to be a date, and he even said he liked her . . .

"What if I ask you to kiss me?"

He let out a low moan. "Ask me and you'll find out."

She bit her bottom lip. If they kissed, what would that mean? Would he regret it the next day? Would she regret it? Would he even like the way she kissed? He probably kissed so many other women, women who were more attractive, more successful, more—

"Ask me." His voice cut through her thoughts, more demanding than ever. He picked up her hand again and squeezed it firmly. "Ask me to kiss you."

She looked at his lips. They were so full, so firm, so close. "W-will you kiss —?"

Before she could even finish talking, he pressed his lips softly to hers, moving them carefully. He released her hand and cupped her neck, placing his other hand on the side of her face, pulling her in even closer as the kiss deepened. He moved his lips over hers, again and again, slowly and controlled, but the growl that escaped his throat sounded like he was about to break loose at any second.

If she had known how amazing his kiss would be, she'd have kissed him that night when they were both in his office. She kissed him back harder now, moving her lips against his.

Her chest dropped as he started to pull away.

She wasn't ready for it to end. Not yet. She reached up to his face to pull his head close, but he still managed to separate his lips from hers. He angled his head back slightly, his forehead touching hers but leaving their lips slightly apart.

She gasped for breath as her stomach sank. "Are you ok?" She could barely hear herself talk over the loud beating of her heart.

His lips brushed against hers as he spoke. "I liked that more than you realize."

"Then why did you stop?"

He touched his lips against hers for one last, brief kiss before pulling away fully. "I think we have an audience."

Ashley jumped away as though she'd been struck by lightning. She stared at his eyes and then timidly glanced around the room.

He was right. There was an audience. A very loud audience that she had somehow forgotten. As soon as she looked up to the kitchen, the staff started cheering and hooting.

Ashley's face started burning. She wanted to run away from that room as soon as possible. With Michael.

CHAPTER 25

Michael sat up in bed two hours before his alarm went off the next morning. His muscles ached from tossing and turning all night. He barely slept.

What was he thinking last night? Had he learned nothing from medical school? Dating didn't work for him. He couldn't be a doctor and be in a relationship. The cost of dating was too steep.

He turned on the shower, letting the water run cold. He needed to clear his brain, so he shed his clothes and stepped in. It was frigid and gave him the jolt he needed. He tensed his muscles, resolving to stay under the cold stream and not adjust the temperature.

He managed to wash his hair and body before his fingers started going numb. He stepped out of the shower, shivering slightly, and walked back to his bedroom. He groaned. The cold shower hadn't worked. He glanced at his phone to check the temperature outside. The mornings were still generally chilly, and this morning was no exception. He put on a sweatshirt, a pair of gym shorts, and his running shoes.

With any luck, the run would work better than the cold

shower. There was a steep hill a mile from his apartment, which was perfect for sprinting up and down. He headed in that direction, accelerating from a jog to a sprint. He would probably be winded before he even reached the hill.

He needed to get to that hill. His mind was already starting to go into overdrive, and he needed to push those thoughts out. Run until it was too hard to think. Needed to gain some focus and control.

He couldn't keep thinking about Ashley and their date. Their kiss. He thought he could handle dating her. How could he have been so blind? He should have just let her continue to think that he was the shallow doctor who talked down to her at work. He should have let her just live her own life without trying to get her attention or her approval. He should have . . .

He picked up his pace even more, pounding the pavement with his feet. No one was out at this time of morning to witness his punishing run—no one to witness his pain.

There was no good way to end things with Ashley now. He couldn't imagine hurting her, but he also couldn't be with her. He had tried dating in the past. He didn't want to be alone forever, but the truth was that people depended on him for survival. If he didn't have a laser-like focus on work, people would die.

How could he have a sharp focus when Ashley's mere presence took control of his every thought?

He rounded the last corner before reaching the bottom of the steep hill and stopped suddenly. A large barricade blocked the road. Construction. He leaned forward and placed his hands on his knees to catch his breath. The side-walk and street were all torn up. Even if he ignored the barricade and ran around it, he'd surely sprain an ankle if he tried to run on the rough and uneven street.

His muscles started to ache from the sudden stop and the

cold air. He needed to do something. The tightening in his chest was probably from running, but it didn't feel right. He needed to start moving again before something bad happened. He needed to stay in control. He needed to keep the panic attack away.

He turned around and started jogging again, letting his muscles stretch. The surrounding streets weren't nearly as steep as the one that was closed for construction. He ran up one street and then another, as fast as he could, but the hills weren't enough of a challenge. His legs and lungs weren't burning enough. He needed something more if he was going to block his thoughts.

Were there any steep hills by Ashley's apartment? Her place was a few miles away from his, but he could probably manage the run there and back. Would she be awake this early? He could stop by a coffee shop near her place and surprise her with an early morning coffee. She probably looked cute when she woke up in the morning with messy hair and—he shook his head and turned down another street, running in the opposite direction from where she lived.

He could find a way to make things work. He could find that balance between managing work and having a personal life. Other people did it. He could do it too.

CHAPTER 26

Ashley stood in the main living room of an empty apartment available for rent and looked around. The woman standing next to her was chewing gum loudly and focused more on her phone than on helping Ashley. She sighed and looked around again.

The carpeting was old, and the paint faded. A section of ceiling had been patched poorly after a leak, and there was a draft coming in through the small window.

She sighed and walked further into the unit. The kitchen wasn't any better. Two cabinets with broken doors hung next to the sink, which offered little counter space. A small fridge and a stove with two burners instead of four filled the rest of the wall space. She cracked open the oven door. It was so small that she doubted she could fit a standard baking sheet in there. She'd be lucky if it actually got hot enough to roast any vegetables.

She wandered back through the empty living room, which would also have to function as the dining room. She could possibly fit a table in here that would be large enough for cooking prep, but then there would be no room for a couch.

The bedroom wasn't much better. At least it had a small window which would give her a view of the street below. Some thick curtains might block out some of the street noise, but she'd probably have to start sleeping with a white-noise machine or earplugs.

The only thing that she almost liked about the apartment was the price. It was still more than her current rent, but it was cheaper than anything else she'd been able to find so far. At least she didn't have to make any decisions today. The apartment would probably still be available for a few more days, so she could keep looking.

She walked back to the living room and pasted on a smile for the landlord. "Thanks for showing me the place."

"You gonna rent it?" The woman turned to leave without taking her eyes off her phone.

"Maybe. I, umm, I'm going to think about it."

"Don't wait too long because I have a lot of interest in this unit. It will be off the market before you know."

"Hmm." Somehow, Ashley doubted that. No one would rent that apartment unless they were all out of options, like her.

She walked down the street to the bus stop, hands in her pockets. That was another perk of this apartment. It was close to the bus stop. Her car still wasn't fixed, and with the rent of this apartment, she wouldn't be able to afford any repairs for a few months.

She sighed. If the bus wasn't running late, she'd still have enough time to stop by the hospital and visit Henry before going back to her apartment to meet Michael. Henry would be happy to hear about their date last night. She'd never met an old man who was as interested in gossip as him.

Was she going to mention the kiss? She'd never been the type of person to kiss-and-tell, but that kiss was amazing. It was almost good enough to make her believe that he didn't care that she was poor and struggling while he was nearly perfect.

The bus pulled up and she got on. There was an empty seat towards the back, next to a window, so she took it. As the bus started moving, she looked around. This was a new area of the city to her. She might as well try to scope out the neighborhood from the bus in case this was to become her new home. There wasn't anything too interesting. A small convenience store, a gas station, a small park, a billboard advertising *Harvest House*, featuring a large picture of Chef Jeff holding a plate of food.

She groaned and squeezed her eyes closed. Was this a sign from the universe? If it was, then the universe had better be a bit more clear. Was the billboard a sign that she should rent the apartment? Give Michael a chance? Or . . .

There was no way she could think about interviewing with Chef Jeff for a cook position.

CHAPTER 27

Ashley's phone buzzed as she stepped onto the inpatient unit of the hospital. Her heart skipped a beat. She stopped midstep and dug through her purse until she found her phone. She bit her lip and tried to ignore the tingling in her chest.

She grabbed her phone and accepted the call without looking at the caller ID. *Don't sound too excited. Play it cool. Be calm.*

"Hello?" She cringed. She didn't even recognize her own voice.

"Ashley, I need you to come to work now. When can you be there?" Gwen's voice bellowed out from her phone.

Her heart stopped fluttering. "I can't work today." She looked around the hallways. Was Gwen in the hospital?

"Ashley, I wouldn't call you if I didn't need you to work today. Cancel your plans if needed. Steve didn't show up for work, and I don't have anyone to cover his shift in the inpatient unit. Come to work today or I'll consider this your two-week notice."

Ashley's hand started shaking. Could Gwen do this?

Could she actually fire her over this? It wasn't like she was on the schedule to work. She glanced around again. She could risk telling Gwen that she wasn't coming to work, but she was already in the hospital, and there was no way to know if Gwen was also here. If she refused and then ran into Gwen on her way out of the hospital, there was no way she'd have a job tomorrow.

She squeezed her eyes closed and gritted her teeth. "I'm already here. I'll start work in five minutes."

"Fine." Gwen hung up without even thanking Ashley for agreeing to work today.

There was only one thing left to do. Ashley opened up her texts on her phone.

Michael, I'm stuck at work today. I have to cancel our plans today. Sorry.

She waited a few minutes but there was no response.

Michael picked up his phone for the tenth time and started writing a text before deleting it, again. He should be glad that Ashley canceled their plans for that afternoon. That was what he wanted. He wanted the space and distance to focus on his work, not on her.

So why couldn't he even think of a response to her text? *Thanks for letting me know*—too casual and cold. *I'll miss you, are you free tomorrow?*—too strong, that would scare her away. *When can I see you again? I'm dying for another kiss*—too truthful and desperate.

This was his chance to mess things up with her. If he

really couldn't have a relationship, he could say something that would definitely scare her away, and then he could go back to his normal life, where he just focused on work and nothing else got in the way. Or, he could be a jerk and make her angry enough that she refused to give him another chance. But even thinking about that made him feel sick to his stomach.

Did men even spend this much time agonizing over what to text someone? He stood up and started pacing in his office. Since when did he have so much trouble figuring out how to communicate? He could sit in front of a patient and explain a complicated heart problem in basic terms, but he couldn't figure out how to talk with the woman who had taken over his thoughts.

He walked over to his open office door and closed it firmly. If she was in the hospital today, he was not going to leave his office until he left for home. He wasn't on-call this weekend, so there should be no reason for him to go into other parts of the hospital. He could stay in his office, do his work, and not run into Ashley.

He picked his phone up again and texted her. *Ok. Last night was nice. I'll call you later this week.* It was a good text. Not too distant, but not committing to anything.

He turned off his phone and went back to his computer.

Hours later, he looked up from his work. The sunlight was fading. She must have left work by now. He left his phone on the desk and tightened the laces on his running shoes before leaving the office to race up and down the hospital stairs again.

CHAPTER 28

Michael finished rinsing off the sweat in his private shower. The hospital where he'd interned only had showers in the physician locker rooms and break rooms, not in the physician's offices. He thought the private bathroom with shower was a bit excessive and unnecessary when he was first hired at this hospital. Within the first month, however, he realized just how nice it was to have a private space to wash off the stress after a difficult surgery.

He toweled off and looked at the pile of gym clothes on the floor. They were covered with sweat. He usually kept an extra pair of clothes in his office since there wasn't enough storage space for clothing in his private bathroom. He hesitated, then wrapped his towel around his waist and headed for the door.

A loud shout rang out as soon as he stepped into his office. He glanced over at his desk and saw the last thing he expected.

Ashley.

What was she doing there? In his office? The first time she'd caught him in a towel was amusing. But this time . . .

He'd spent all day trying to focus on anything except her. How was he supposed to tamper his feelings for her when she was sitting by his desk and he was wearing nothing but a towel, again?

"Ashley . . ." the words stuck in his throat.

She stared at him, mouth hanging open. "Again? Don't you ever wear clothes in here? I mean, I wouldn't have . . . I didn't mean—your door was open. I was just going to leave you a note." She held up the sticky note pad on his desk and showed him where she had made some marks. She glanced back at it and crumpled it up before sticking it in her pocket.

He didn't have the energy to wonder what she had written. All he needed to do was focus on controlling himself. He took a few steps to the large cabinet on the opposite side of his office. Even with his back to her, her look was making his skin tingle.

"Should I leave?" She spoke quietly.

He sighed. His confusion was his problem, not hers. "Give me a minute to put on clothes. Stay." He turned around and saw the confusion in her face. "Stay," he repeated, more firmly this time.

He waited for her to nod before he went back to the bathroom and put on his clothes. He didn't have time for another cold shower, but he rinsed his face with cold water before returning to his office.

She was no longer sitting at his desk but had moved over to the couch and was studying her hands.

"I didn't think you were working today. I just came by to leave you a note. I thought your door was open from cleaning. But I guess that doesn't really make sense since we don't clean the offices on the weekend."

She looked uncomfortable sitting there. He wanted to do something, make her feel more at ease. He sat down next to her and placed his arm on the back of the couch. Close enough to make his heart start beating wildly but not quite touching her.

"I'm glad you came by." The words came out of his mouth before he could stop them. But it was true. His mind was still racing, but the tightness that was in his chest all day had disappeared.

She glanced at him and gave him a small smile. "Are you ok? You sound a little . . . off."

He pressed his lips together. How could she read him so clearly?

"I'm just having a rough day."

"Anything I can help you with?"

He looked at her closely. How could she possibly help him when she was the source of his pain? He sat up and placed a hand on her shoulder. "Have you been working all afternoon?"

She nodded.

"Turn around. I'll rub your shoulders and back."

She gave him a quizzical look but turned so her back was to him. He tentatively reached out and then started rubbing her shoulders. What was he doing? He thought it would be easier to control his emotions if he wasn't looking at her directly, but now it was even harder. All he wanted to do was take care of her, make her happy, earn her affection and trust.

"That feels amazing." She sighed. "I was so annoyed when Gwen called me in to work today. I would have said no, but I was already at the hospital when she called, and she threatened to fire me. She's really horrible. I would rather cook all day than clean."

He found a knot on her shoulder and started massaging it. "Tell me if I hurt you," he said, referring to the massage. She didn't respond immediately. He ached to ask her something but hesitated. If he asked her, he might scare her and push her away. But would that be a bad thing? If she were to run away at this point, he wouldn't have to work so hard to find a way to manage work and a relationship.

He decided to take the chance. "If you'd rather cook than clean, why don't you quit? Why don't you at least interview with Jeff?"

He felt her tense under his hands. He shifted his hands slightly and ran his thumb gently over the nape of her neck before resuming the massage.

"Some things are complicated."

He sighed. "I guess so." He should know. He was stuck in a complicated mess right now.

She sat in silence for a minute before speaking again. "It's just that I don't know you well enough to get into all the details. But it's not as easy as just quitting my job and getting a new one. It's just . . . well, it's complicated."

He gave her shoulders a squeeze and moved his hand slightly as he continued to massage. "Would it help if I told you something about myself?" He must have overworked himself with exercise today. That was the only explanation. Why else would he willingly offer to let her get even closer?

"There is something that I've wondered about," she asked in a soft voice.

"Go ahead."

"How do you handle all the stress of being a cardiologist? I mean, you actually hold people's hearts in your hands when you do surgery. How do you do that, day after day?"

He shrugged. "You get used to the stress."

"Oh." She didn't really sound convinced by his answer.

He thought for a minute. Did she want the real truth? Did he even want to tell her? Very few people knew about his panic attacks. He wanted to tell her everything about himself. He wanted her to be part of his life. There was something about her that made him want to open up. She wasn't the type of person who would laugh in his face or tell other people about his weakness. But what woman would want to date a man who admitted to having panic attacks?

A lightbulb went off in his head. No woman would want to date someone who had panic attacks. That's all he had to do. Admit out loud that he had panic attacks, and she would run away. He wouldn't have to carry around any guilt about hurting her. She would be the one to leave, and he could return to his uncomplicated life.

He took a deep breath in and focused on massaging another tense muscle in her back. "I don't always handle the stress well. I get panic attacks. Never when I'm with a patient or in surgery, but sometimes later. When I have time to think about things, or I feel like I'm not doing enough as a doctor, I get overwhelmed, and the panic attacks start." He gritted his teeth. The damage was done.

"Panic attacks are horrible. I used to get them too." She turned around, brushing his hands off her back. "Turn around. It's my turn to rub your back."

He clenched his jaw. He just told her that he got panic attacks, and her response was to offer to massage his shoulders?

He turned around. If she wasn't scared off yet, he'd have to push her further. She placed her hands on his shoulders tentatively. He shuddered briefly from her touch. He ached to turn back around and kiss her, but he needed to remain focused.

"W-why did you get panic attacks?" He cleared his throat. This was pathetic. He could barely speak when she was touching him.

She spoke slowly. "I struggled after my parents died. Didn't think I could manage on my own."

He held himself rigid, refusing to turn around and gather her in his arms. "I'm sorry that happened."

She continued rubbing his back harder. "I had panic attacks because I felt alone."

She sounded defeated. He couldn't fight with himself any longer. He turned around and grabbed her hands, pulling her in close. She let out a small gasp.

"You aren't alone anymore." He placed his hand on her cheek, drawing her face in close to his.

"I know," she whispered. "I have Emily and Kelly as my family now." She bit her lower lip and placed her hand on top of his.

"You can count on me, too, if you want." He leaned in closer. There was no use fighting it anymore—he couldn't. He wasn't going to chase her away. Instead, he was going to hold her tight and make things work. He wrapped his other hand around her upper arm and drew her closer.

He brushed his lips against hers, slowly and tentatively at first, but when she placed her hand on his shoulder, grabbing at his shirt and pulling his chest against her, he deepened the kiss. She leaned into him and moved her lips against his. It wasn't enough. He needed more. He ran his fingers through her hair, letting them get tangled.

This was what he had needed all day. No matter how long or fast he ran, he'd never be able to replace the longing he had for her touch.

She let out a quiet whimper and pushed him back, separating her lips from his. She blinked her eyes several times and then shook her head as if to clear her thoughts. She stood up and backed away to the door.

"I have to go."

Michael groaned and leaned forward, placing his head in his hands. He'd messed up. He'd pushed too hard. He'd scared her away.

CHAPTER 29

Monday morning came too quickly. Ashley scrolled through her emails as she sat at a table in the staff room for a fifteen-minute break. No emails about graduate school. No email notifications about apartments to rent.

She logged onto an apartment hunting website and filled out the familiar search bar, complete with preferred rent and amenities. She left all the amenity options blank. She'd be lucky to find a livable apartment with a kitchen. There was no need to dream about having a dishwasher or washing machine in her unit. A door with a lock in a safe neighborhood and a nearby bus stop was the most she could ask for. And there were no guarantees that she'd be able to find one fitting that bill.

No new apartments appeared in the search results.

She thought about the apartment she visited the other day. Could she really survive in an apartment that didn't have a full-sized stove and oven? And no prep space for any food?

It didn't matter. She couldn't afford the rent on that apartment.

Why hadn't she heard anything from the last graduate school on her list? If she did get in, then it would make more sense to start looking for an apartment near the college campus. She'd also have to figure out the amount of money due for tuition and fees. Loans and grants would help to cover most of that and help with paying for an apartment.

She pulled up the apartment search engine again and typed in a different location. What were the apartments like in the area surrounding Chef Jeff's restaurant? She increased the monthly rent range just out of curiosity. It never hurt to look and imagine. It was like window shopping at Tiffany's, but for apartments instead of jewelry.

A few listings appeared in the results. One had a communal rooftop deck with barbecues. She always wanted to try her skills with grilling. Another had barbecues and a large pool. The last apartment featured a walkout balcony and views over the river. She looked at the prices. She'd never afford that amount on her minimum wage salary.

This was pointless. She might as well search for million-dollar homes for sale. There was as much chance of her paying the downpayment on a million-dollar estate as there was affording one of the apartments on that list.

The break room door opened, and Ashley looked up as Kelly entered.

"Hey, Kelly."

Kelly walked over to Ashley and sat down. "Bring in any treats today?"

Ashley shrugged. "Been too busy."

"Hmph. So tell me, how was the date?" She leaned in close, looking eager.

Ashley shifted uncomfortably. "The date was good. We went to Harvest House, and the food was even better than I imagined."

"I don't care about the food. How were things with Michael?"

"Umm . . . good. I mean, he was really nice and amazing and . . ." Ashley took a deep breath. "The date couldn't have gone better."

"Details, please! Did you kiss?"

"Kelly!" Ashley shushed her, even though there was no one else in the room. She leaned forward and whispered. "Yes."

"Good for you! It's about time you go for something you want, and you obviously wanted him. Don't hold back any details. Did you see him again this weekend?"

Ashley looked down and nodded. "Gwen called me into work on Saturday. I ran into him by mistake in his office, and . . ."

Kelly tapped the table with her hands impatiently while Ashley gathered her thoughts.

"It was weird. At first, we were having a really good conversation, and I felt like I was finally seeing him clearly. I don't know why, but I felt like I could trust him. You know that feeling you get when you just want to be with someone? All day long, I just wanted to see him again, and then, once we started talking, it felt like everything was right with the world." She looked down, her cheeks starting to burn. "But I think I ruined things between us."

"Oh, honey, I'm sure it isn't as bad as you think. What happened?" Kelly's voice was thick with concern.

"I kissed him, or maybe he kissed me. I don't know which way it happened, but we kissed. And then I freaked out and ran."

"What did he say?"

"He said nothing. I actually got up and left as soon as we stopped kissing."

Kelly inhaled quietly. "Have you seen him since then?"

"No. I also haven't texted or called him, and he hasn't contacted me. I think it's over between us."

"Ash, it's not over until it's actually over. Why don't you just call him and explain?"

"What is there to explain?"

"Do you want to be with him?"

She shrugged.

Kelly sighed loudly. "Ashley, I'm going to tell you something that you might not like, but I'm only going to say it because you are like a daughter to me."

Ashley hung her head. Kelly had only given her a talk once before, and she knew better than to try to avoid it.

"I've watched you sit by and wait for a graduate school to accept you. I've watched you waste your talent as a cook because I always figured that, sooner or later, you'd find the path you were meant to travel. But this . . . this is too much. A man like Michael won't be available forever. You've got to start figuring out what it is that you want, and go for it."

She paused to catch her breath. Ashley waited to see if she was done. After a minute of silence, she decided it was safe to speak. "Chef Jeff offered to let me interview for a job at his restaurant."

Kelly smacked the table lightly. "It's about time you took your cooking talent seriously. When's the interview?"

"I didn't agree to interview."

Kelly's head dropped, and she spoke softly, with concern. "Do you really want to stay here forever and end up like Gwen? Or keep chasing graduate school? Is that going to make you happy?"

Ashley blinked hard. "I don't know. I'm just confused. It's complicated."

"Honey, sooner or later, I hope you decide to trust me, or anyone really, enough to talk about why it's so complicated."

Ashley's phone started buzzing. She looked at the screen,

and her eyes started to sting. "It's Gwen. My break time ended five minutes ago. I have to run."

Kelly nodded. "I'm here for you if you ever need anything. You know I love you as if you were my own child."

Ashley nodded and tried to swallow the lump forming in her throat. "I know."

CHAPTER 30

Ashley spent the rest of the afternoon avoiding Michael. It wasn't hard since she was working on the pediatric floor, and Michael's patients were all adults. But only while in the locker room at the end of her shift did Ashley feel like she could breathe again. She looked at her phone one last time before closing her locker door.

There were no missed calls or texts.

Shouldn't he have reached out to her by now? Was he trying to give her space to sort out her confusion, or had he finally given up on her as a lost cause?

It wouldn't really be a surprise if he'd given up on her. He was a distraction, anyway. If it weren't for him, she wouldn't need to think about chasing her dream to be a chef and essentially betray her parents. He was the one who pushed her into meeting Chef Jeff, and he was the one who was pushing her to interview for the job at his restaurant. Now Kelly was also on her case about working in the restaurant. Why wouldn't either of them just let her live her life the way she needed to live it?

They didn't have to face the look of disappointment on

her parents' face when she told them that she was going to drop out of college and enroll in culinary school. They didn't have to argue with them about all the reasons to finish her undergrad degree in social work. They didn't wake up to a phone call from the hospital, telling her that her mother was dead and that her father wasn't going to last much longer. They didn't have to live each day with the knowledge that her parents died just hours after the worst fight of their lives, all because she wanted to become a chef instead of finishing her undergraduate degree and following in her parents' footsteps.

She walked out of the locker room to the staircase at the end of the hall, and started to descend. She still needed to think about that ugly apartment. She should just sign the lease for that place, even though she'd have to pick up extra shifts each month in order to afford the rent. She could consider it punishment for the way she'd messed up her life so much, first by disappointing her parents and now by pushing Michael away.

She reached the landing for the second floor and froze. Michael was standing in the middle of the steps below, staring at her. She reached her hand up and smoothed her hair. If this was their last conversation together, then she might as well look as good as she could after spending the last eight hours cleaning.

"Hey, Michael."

"Ashley." His voice was deeper than usual. He shifted slightly. "Heading home?"

"Yes."

"Is your car fixed already?"

She shook her head. "I'm taking the bus."

He frowned. "I'll drive you home."

"You don't have to."

He ran his hand over his jaw. "I want to." He raised the jacket that he was carrying. "I'm on my way out anyway."

"I can take care of myself. I don't need your help to get home." She walked down the last few steps and tried to walk past him.

He stepped to the side and blocked her path. He reached out and arranged his jacket around her shoulders. "It's pretty cold outside. I don't want you to freeze, and your jacket doesn't look very warm."

She inhaled deeply, enjoying his scent. "I can handle the cold." She bit her lip. He still wasn't moving.

He cleared his throat. "Can we just talk for a minute?"

She sighed. "About what?"

He reached out gingerly and hesitated. He drew his hand back and placed it in his pants pocket. "I don't know what to do about you. I can't stop thinking about you. I just want to be with you. But . . ."

Ashley shuddered. Were they really going to officially end things in the stairwell of the hospital? It was one of the most depressing places she could think of for a breakup. Grey cement steps, grey cement walls, grey railings, musty smell of antiseptic and stale air. This needed to be over quickly so she wouldn't miss her bus.

"I know. It's fine. We can end things now before they get too messy."

"What are you talking about?" His voice was strained. He reached out again and grasped her upper arms gently. "I'm not ending things. That's the opposite of what I want to do. I just need to know that you are in this too. I keep thinking that I'm going to scare you away, and I need to know that you want this as much as I do. I need to know that you'll stop running away from me. I— I—" He let go of her arms and took a step back, running his fingers through his hair. He turned, then shook his head and started pacing.

Ashley frowned. "I don't know what to say."

He turned back to her, his eyes intense. Her breath caught in her throat, and she took a step away, her back brushing up to the cold wall. "Tell me right now if I should walk away and leave you alone. Or tell me if you want this as much as I want this. I'm going crazy. I can't think of anything except you."

Ashley wet her lips. "I keep waiting for you to change your mind and realize that you should be with someone else."

"There is no one else I want."

Her stomach started doing somersaults. "Same."

"What?" He took a step closer, removing any distance between them.

"I want you. I want to be with you too."

"Then it's official? We are dating? Boyfriend and girlfriend?"

The corners of Ashley's mouth started to rise of their own accord. "Do people our age really say that? It sounds like we're in high school or something."

He groaned. "I don't care. Is that a yes?"

Ashley sighed and looked directly in his eyes. "There's one condition."

His eyes darkened.

"You don't ask me to be a chef again. You don't ask me to interview at your friend's restaurant. Cooking is just a hobby, and you don't ask me about it again." She tried to cross her arms, but he was standing too close and didn't budge. She rested her hand on his bicep instead. If he didn't agree, they could have no future.

His Adam's apple bobbed as he swallowed hard. He exhaled loudly, then nodded. "I won't do that."

She started to grin. "Then it's official."

He leaned in close. "Should we seal the deal with a kiss?"

"Definitely." She barely finished the word before his lips were on hers, kissing her. She'd never made out before in the hospital staircase. If Gwen saw her, she'd probably be fired. But then again, Gwen was always trying to fire her. It was worth the risk to feel his mouth pressed against hers for a few more seconds.

She wrapped her arms around his neck just seconds before he ended the kiss. She frowned. "Give me a ride home?"

He smiled. "Let's head to your place."

CHAPTER 31

Ashley tapped on the open door to Gwen's windowless office. Gwen looked up, eyebrows creased. That was as much of an invitation as Ashley could expect. She stepped inside cautiously and sat down in the cracked chair opposite Gwen's desk.

Nothing could ruin her day today. Not when things were finally working out between her and Michael. She felt stronger than ever before. Almost immune to Gwen's influence.

She cleared her throat and focused on controlling her facial expression. Steady and calm was the best way to ask Gwen for a favor. "I talked with Rachel, and she and I would like to formally switch main assignments. Specifically, she wants to take over my primary shifts in the cardiac units while I take over her shifts in the oncology wards."

Gwen crossed her arms, leaned back in her chair, and said nothing.

Ashley clasped her hands on her lap. "It's just that she and I both want to switch, and since we work the same hours, it won't create too much extra work for you to rearrange the shifts."

Gwen remained silent. Ashley couldn't read her face. It was as blank as a brick wall.

She held her breath, waiting. This was the last little hurdle to jump through. She thought about Michael's look last night when he left her apartment and sat up a little straighter.

Finally, Gwen blinked and pursed her lips. "Was this your idea, or Rachel's?"

"Mine, but she said that she'd like to switch." That wasn't completely a lie. It was actually Michael who asked her if she would consider changing cleaning areas in the hospital. He said he'd feel awkward asking her to clean up his exam rooms in between patients. Rachel was willing to switch in exchange for some peanut butter brownies next week, but that was hardly a bribe. She would have baked the brownies for Rachel even if she wasn't asking for a favor.

"Fine." Gwen looked down at her desk and jotted something on a paper before glancing back up at Ashley. "Rachel can switch primary units if she wants. Tell her to let me know by the end of the day which unit she wants."

Ashley's heart leapt. "So I can switch to oncology?" She tried to keep the smile from spreading across her face.

Gwen stared at her, eyes unblinking. "No. You're fired."

Ashley froze, her mouth stuck somewhere between a smile and shock. Her chest tightened like all the oxygen had been sucked out of the room. She moved her head forward and tried to focus. "W-what?"

"You heard me. Have your locker cleaned out by the end of the day and turn in your badge to security on the way out. Your last paycheck will be mailed to you in two weeks. That's all." Gwen turned away from Ashley and shuffled through a pile of papers.

Ashley sat for a moment because she didn't trust her legs to support her. Gwen had finally done it. Finally fired her. It was over. She was a failure. And now everyone else would know.

She pursed her lips together and studied Gwen's face. The woman didn't care that she ruined everything. She sat behind that desk like she ruled over a cleaning empire. She didn't.

Ashley stood up and balled her fists. "Why do you hate me so much? You've been trying to fire me for months, and I haven't done anything wrong!"

Gwen didn't look up. "I don't hate you. It's not personal. You were late last week. You are clumsy and waste time cleaning up messes that you make. One of the cardiac clinic nurses, Theresa, let me know that last week, you caused a delay in their patient schedule because you spilled a bucket of water when you should have been cleaning up vomit in an exam room. She also let me know that you were making out in a stairwell yesterday." Gwen's voice was as cold as ice and devoid of any emotion.

"You can't fire me for what I do when I'm not on the clock!"

"Doesn't matter. You wasted an entire container of medical supplies when you spilled them on the floor last month. You broke a vacuum two months ago, and a package of tissue boxes were destroyed when you spilled a bucket of water. A stack of patient robes had to be rewashed when you spilled hand soap on them. A box of gloves was destroyed when —"

"Fine. I made mistakes. But I've never missed a shift. I've never complained about last-minute changes to my schedule. I've come in on weekends and evenings to cover for other people. That has to count for something." Ashley spoke firmly, willing her voice not to crack.

"You already said that. I considered your past performance, which is why you weren't fired weeks ago. But now I've changed my mind." Gwen's voice remained flat and bored as if she was discussing an upcoming budget meeting instead of someone's livelihood.

"What's the real reason?"

Gwen finally broke her frozen expression and looked away. She almost looked guilty.

Ashley sat back down, her mind made up. "I'm not leaving this office until I get the real answer. You've been threatening to fire me for months, and I have the right to know why you are firing me now."

A shadow crept over Gwen's face. She wouldn't look directly at Ashley and focused on the wall behind her. "Arguing with me won't change my mind."

"Then tell me why you decided to fire me when you're already short-staffed and can barely get all the shifts covered."

Gwen finally looked at Ashley again with the familiar, disapproving glare that she must have perfected years ago, judging by the way the wrinkles were etched around her mouth and eyes. Ashley stared back. She wasn't going to break eye contact first. Either she or Gwen would crack first, and it wasn't going to be her.

After an eternity, Gwen finally looked away. "Fine, Ashley. You really want answers?" Gwen's face changed, and she looked tired. Ashley nodded. Gwen's face stiffened again, and when she spoke, her voice was as sharp as steel. "You are fired because you don't belong in housekeeping. You were the worst cleaner I had on staff. I made a mistake by not firing you a long time ago. Stop by Human Resources on your way out to complete the paperwork for your severance pay."

Ashley felt like she'd been slapped. She was mad. "Gwen—"

"Do I need to call security to escort you out?"

Ashley's words caught in her throat. The fight was clearly over. Gwen won.

She stood up, gave Gwen one last glare, and left.

CHAPTER 32

Ashley hung up her phone and turned on the living room light. The sun sank below the horizon twenty minutes ago, and she had no job leads. No hospitals were hiring cleaners.

It was time to start calling hotels. She pulled up the search engine on her phone and searched for local hotels. There were a lot in the city. One of them must be hiring.

She tapped on the phone number for the first hotel that appeared on her screen. An automated message greeted her. She listened closely to the menu options.

To book a room, press one. To speak with the front desk, press two.

What she needed was an option for getting your life out of the dumpster.

She pressed two and waited until she heard a bored voice answer.

"Hotel By the Bay, this is Brennon."

She swallowed hard. "Hi, are you hiring cleaners?"

"I don't know."

"Is there a manager around who can help?"

"He left for the night. You can call again tomorrow."

"Oh. Ok." She squeezed her eyes closed. "Do you know of any place that's hiring cleaners?"

"Is that the only thing you can do?" Brennon's voice became slightly less bored.

"What do you mean?"

"You called here. Hotel By the Bay."

"Yes, because I'm looking for a job. Cleaning."

"Right." Even over the phone, sarcasm dripped from his voice. "You called the Hotel By the Bay for a cleaning job. How old are you?"

"What's that supposed to mean?" Something in the tone of Brennon's voice made Ashley's stomach churn.

"Do I have to spell it out for you?"

"Yes."

Brennon waited a minute before he responded. "Forget it. Call back tomorrow if you are actually interested in working here."

Ashley pulled the phone back from her ear and looked at the screen. He'd hung up on her. The search engine results for local hotels lit up her screen. She lifted a finger, then pressed the link for the hotel's website.

A picture appeared of a two-story motel with grey cinderblock walls and a parking lot filled with potholes. A second building stood next to the hotel. Ashley squinted her eyes and pulled the screen closer to her face.

The hotel stood next to a strip club.

She shuddered and moved her fingers quickly, closing the tab for that hotel.

Lesson learned. Look at the website before calling somewhere for a job.

She took a deep breath in. She didn't have to find a new job today. She could sign up for unemployment wages and use her savings to get by until she got a new job. In the meantime, she would look for an apartment.

She called the property management for the apartment she looked at the other day—the tiny, disgusting apartment with the smallest kitchen she'd seen.

"Hello?" The same lady who'd shown her the apartment answered the phone.

"I'm calling about the apartment I saw a few days ago. The one on Mill Street."

"What about it?" She sounded as annoyed today as she sounded a few days ago.

"I want to rent it." Ashley gritted her teeth and forced the words out.

"Fine. Stop by my office tomorrow with proof of employment, your last two months of pay stubs to verify income, and be ready to pay the deposit. I require the first month, last month, and security deposit paid upfront."

Ashley's throat constricted. "I don't have proof of employment. But I'm looking for a job. And you said you only required a one month payment upfront."

"Don't waste my time. I'm not renting to someone who doesn't have a job." The woman's voice changed. Instead of annoyed, she sounded royally upset.

"I'll have one soon. I promise."

"Call me if that happens. And be ready to pay three months rent and security deposit when you sign the lease."

Ashley's jaw hung open. Could she even do that? She swallowed hard and tried to ignore the churning feeling in her stomach. "That's not what you said the other day."

"It's what I'm saying now. Goodbye."

For the second time that evening, Ashley stared at her phone in disbelief.

She needed a break. And a job.

Ashley walked to her kitchen and opened the cupboard door. She had about a cup of flour, half a bag of sugar, and a nearly empty box of baking powder. She didn't have to look in the fridge to know that she was out of milk, butter, and eggs. Not enough of any ingredient to bake anything.

She grabbed her tea kettle. Tea always helped her feel better.

She heard a tap on her front door followed by the sound of her door creaking open and Emily's voice. "Hey Ashley, I'm coming in!"

Ashley turned around and took a few steps until she was back in the living room and could see Emily walking in, holding a large box. "I came here as soon as I could. Well, first I cleared out your locker for you. Also, Rachel and Amy said that they are going to miss you. I could just about kill Theresa and Gwen. They are the worst! I also brought ice cream. Mint chocolate chip and fudge swirl. I didn't know what you'd be in the mood for." Emily paused and looked around for a place to put down the box.

Ashley's stomach churned again uneasily at the thought of eating anything. She glanced at her cousin before turning around to go back to the kitchen. "I'm making tea. Do you want some too? We can dig into the ice cream later."

"Yes, tea would be great." Emily placed the box on the living room floor next to her coffee table. "What's this list?"

Ashley turned around. Emily was holding the list where she'd written and crossed off each hospital, hotel, and store that she'd called to ask about a job.

"Job hunting. No one is hiring." Her voice cracked as she spoke.

"Oh, Ash . . ." Emily walked over and wrapped her in a hug. "Go relax on the couch and let me make your tea."

Ashley hesitated but then walked back to the living room and collapsed on the sofa. The list was back on the coffee table, mocking her. She closed her eyes until Emily came back into the room, two mugs of tea in her hands.

"I called all those places, and no one wants me. I don't

know what to do. I need a job." She took the mug of tea from Emily and inhaled deeply. Chamomile.

"It's only the first day. You have time before you get a new job."

"I can't rent an apartment without proof of income."

"It will happen. You'll find a job. I'll help."

Ashley shrugged. It was hard to remain optimistic.

Emily blew on her tea and took a tentative sip. She kept the mug close to her mouth as she spoke quietly. "Have you looked for any restaurant positions? Or called any catering companies to see if they need cooks?"

Ashley gritted her teeth. She should have known this was coming. "No."

"If no one else is hiring, maybe you should give it a try. Or even start your own business as a personal chef."

"No."

"Ashley, don't you think enough time has—?"

"No."

"Won't you consider—?"

"No. I will not consider it."

Emily frowned and put her mug of tea on the coffee table. She turned and looked directly at Ashley. "Look, don't you think your parents want you to be happy? Haven't you punished yourself enough? You aren't going to change what happened by just ignoring your talent. Do you really think they want you to work in a job that you hate so you can go to school to train for a job you don't want?"

"I want to be a social worker." She wasn't going to back down.

"You don't even like the work." Emily narrowed her eyes at Ashley.

"I might like it."

"You hated your internship last year."

"Anyone would have hated working with Susan as their supervisor."

Emily shrugged. "True. But I knew your parents too, remember? They were my aunt and uncle. They always just wanted you to be happy."

"They weren't happy with me the night that they died." She tried to swallow the lump forming in her throat.

"Look, everyone fights from time to time. Even if they weren't thrilled that you wanted to go to culinary school, they still loved you. They wouldn't want you to be miserable."

Ashley put her tea down and rubbed her forehead. "I can't talk about this now. My head hurts again. Thanks for stopping by, but I think I need to be alone. Maybe I'll go to bed early."

Emily frowned but got up. "Ok. I'll check in on you again tomorrow." She hesitated briefly. "Remember, you can always move in with me until you find a job and an apartment. My place isn't big, but I have a couch that you can use. You'll get through this."

Warmth spread through Ashley's cheeks. "Thanks, Emily. I don't know what I'd do without you."

She watched Emily let herself out and then closed her eyes.

CHAPTER 33

Michael tapped on Ashley's apartment door and waited with a bag of takeout food in one hand and his computer bag slung over his shoulder. He could hear Ashley's voice through the door. It sounded like she was on the phone. He hesitated and knocked again, a little louder. There were some brief rattling sounds of the deadbolt unlocking, and then the door creaked open. Ashley motioned for him to enter and then turned around and walked into her bedroom, closing the door behind him.

Michael closed the apartment door and walked into the kitchen, setting the takeout food containers that he'd brought on the table. Then he went back to the living room and perched on the edge of the couch.

He set his computer up on the coffee table, which creaked and shifted under the weight of the small computer but held steady. Within moments, he pulled up a video tutorial on writing a resume and settled into the couch to watch.

After about ten minutes, Ashley walked out of the bedroom and sat on the couch next to him. "What are you watching?"

"A video about how to write a good resume. I figured it would be helpful." He reached behind him and pulled at the throw blanket on the back of Ashley's couch. He unfolded it and wrapped it around her. "I asked around the department today. Theresa confessed to complaining about you to Gwen. She said she wanted you to get transferred, not fired." He took a deep breath in and braced himself for the next part. "Theresa also asked me out. I turned her down. I told her I can't be with anyone except you."

Ashley's silence filled the room. He looked over at her. She stared back at him.

"Did you really mean that?" Her voice sounded small, uncertain.

He touched her lightly under the chin and turned her head so that he could look directly in her eyes. "I do."

She shivered slightly, and the corners of her mouth turned up, but the smile didn't reach her eyes. He could read the worry in her face and wanted to make it go away.

He turned back to the computer to bookmark the video. "Bill is asking around at his hospital to see if there are any job openings. He said he'll let us know if he hears of any."

"I already called his hospital, and they said they weren't hiring in housecleaning." Ashley's voice sounded strained.

"Well, don't give up yet. In the meantime, we can focus on a great resume. Since we probably can't depend on Gwen to give you a good reference, we need to highlight all your skills on your resume." He pulled up another video on job hunting tips. "We might need to get creative to find you a job, but we'll find something. Are you good at typing? We could look into administrative assistant jobs." He clenched his jaw. He was not going to ask her about Jeff's interview offer. He made a promise. Any restaurant would be lucky to have her on staff, but he wasn't about to lose her trust in him over a job.

But it made no sense. Would she really rather be unemployed and at the brink of homelessness instead of cooking in one of the best restaurants in the city?

Michael pushed his thoughts about Jeff's restaurant out of his head. "Sorry. I know you can do this all on your own and that you'll be fine without my help, but I want to do something."

"This is really nice. I can't believe that you want to help me so much."

"It's nothing, really. I brought over food. Want to eat first, or work first?"

Ashley didn't move. She grabbed the corner of the blanket that he had wrapped around her and started playing with the fabric. "I'm not sure there's much use in looking for jobs tonight. See that list over there?" She pointed to two pieces of paper near his computer, both filled with handwritten lists that had been crossed out. "Those are all the places I called and aren't hiring."

"Don't give up yet."

"I haven't. But, also . . . well, remember that promise you made yesterday? When I asked you not to talk about me becoming a chef?

Michael nodded and held his breath in anticipation.

"I still don't want to talk about it. But, I called Jeff. He wants me to come to the restaurant Saturday morning to interview. He said to bring you along and we can all have lunch together. He made it really clear that he won't hire me just because of our relationship. I'll have to really impress him with my cooking. I still don't know if I could take the job, though, if he offers me one. My parents wouldn't—" she took a deep breath and started her sentence over. "I need to have a job, and I can't make it very long without a paycheck. Even with unemployment, I can't make ends meet long enough to wait for the first unemployment check. My car still won't run, and the restaurant isn't on the bus route, and—"

Michael cut her off. "I'll drive you. Just let me know what time to pick you up."

Ashley looked like a huge weight was lifted off her shoulders. "Ten in the morning."

"How about I pick you up at nine and take you out for breakfast first?" If Ashley was willing to put aside whatever had been stopping her from interviewing for this job, he wanted her to be well fed before stepping into that kitchen.

Ashley nodded, and Michael continued before she could change her mind. "I have good news for you. Your new friend, Henry, was discharged today."

"Really?" Ashley didn't look as happy as he thought she'd look. "That's great."

"What's wrong?"

"I was just hoping to see him again before he was discharged. We talked about getting together this weekend. He doesn't have family nearby, and I don't know if he has any visitors at home. I was going to bring him some food."

"You still can. He left a note for you." He pulled a piece of paper out of his pocket with Henry's phone number and address written in his shaky handwriting. "I guess he found out that we were dating."

"Oh, um, he guessed that the other day when we ate lunch together." The first real smile appeared on Ashley's face as she took the paper from him.

Michael raised his eyebrows teasingly. "Should I be jealous that you finally look happy now that I've given you another man's phone number?"

She picked up a pillow and threw it at him. It hit him square in the face and he laughed. He had finally taken her mind off her troubles, and he was glad to take a pillow in the face if it meant she was happy. He tossed it back to her.

"Watch yourself, Ash, or you—"

"Or what?" She threw the pillow at him again and leapt off the couch, running to the kitchen.

He tossed the pillow on the ground and followed her into the kitchen.

CHAPTER 34

Early Saturday morning, Michael settled himself in a chair in the corner of the restaurant kitchen. True to his promise, he didn't ask Ashley why she was so reluctant to work in a restaurant, but just arrived early at her apartment to take her to breakfast and then drive her to the interview. The table he was seated at was the same one where he and Ashley sat during their date. He offered to sit somewhere else, far away from the kitchen, but Jeff shrugged him off and now handed him a steaming mug of coffee and a plate of biscotti.

He settled down to work on his computer while Ashley and Jeff moved about the kitchen. He could barely read a sentence before glancing back at her. He already loved watching her move around a kitchen. She moved like she was doing a carefully choreographed dance, with sure movements and ease. She used a large knife with skill, and she was more confident than he'd ever seen her. Watching her prepare to cook was like watching an artist prepare to create a masterpiece.

Michael wished he could hear the conversation between Ashley and Jeff as they cooked, but they were talking too quietly. Soon, an enticing aroma of sauteed onions and garlic filled the kitchen, along with other unfamiliar smells. He watched in amazement as she placed one pan after another filled with food on the large cooktop while placing others in the oven.

He lost count of how many items she was cooking at once. This was the woman he'd been dreaming about, the one he couldn't remove from his mind. He had known there was something more to her lurking below the surface. He had seen hints of her passion and confidence in the times they'd been together, one on one. This was the same woman who, only weeks before, seemed too shy to talk with anyone at work. Never had Michael seen her look as happy and confident as she looked in that moment.

A satisfied smile crossed her face as she tasted something that was simmering on the stove. Michael longed to have that smile remain on her face. In that moment, he knew that she was someone remarkable, unique. Someone who he did not want to let go of. Someone he was falling for, hard.

He stretched his arms out, looking at the clock in surprise to see that another hour had passed by with him watching her cook. He realized that he could easily spend his entire day watching her in her element, doing what she so clearly loved to do.

With a sigh, he was dragged back to reality by the buzzing of his phone. He glanced at Ashley to see if she noticed the disruption, but she was too focused on her work to notice anything else.

He looked at the number on the caller ID. It was the hospital.

"Hello, this is Dr. Tobers."

"Hi, th-this is Dr. Peter Emmit, third-year medical student." Michael waited for what would come next. He wasn't on call this weekend.

"It's about your patient, um…Henry Watts."

Michael sat up, alert. "What about him?"

"The attending doctor told me to contact you. I know you aren't on call this weekend, but he told me to . . ."

"What's going on with Henry?" Michael snapped at the medical student and didn't care. If one of his patients was in trouble, he needed to know immediately.

"His condition is worsening. They need you at the hospital. We had to perform a code blue on him, but he was resuscitated."

Michael swore under his breath. He grabbed his computer, tossed it in his bag, and looked around him. "Call me back in five minutes with an update on him. I'm on my way, will be there in half an hour."

He hung up on the medical student and glanced at Ashley. There was no way he could wait to leave until she finished her interview. He had to be at the hospital as soon as possible. His heart skipped a beat as he thought of how much he wanted to stay there, watching her every move. But he was a doctor. He had responsibilities to people other than himself. Minutes could make the difference between life or death, and he was wasting valuable time.

"Ashley." His voice sounded rough even to his own ears. She broke out of her concentration, looking up at him as though she forgot anyone was in the room. She gave him a beaming smile. His heart broke as the smile faded from her face. "Emergency at the hospital, I have to leave. If I'm not back by the time you are done, you'll have to . . ." He paused, lost for words at the thought of disappointing and abandoning her.

"It's ok. Go do what you need to do. I can take the bus. I'll get home on my own." She gave him a confident smile again. "Go save lives, doctor." She blew him a kiss.

He took one last longing look at her, torn between

wanting to support her and the demands of his job. His heart sank as his phone started buzzing again in his hand. Michael answered the phone as he turned his back on Ashley and walked out of the restaurant, listening to the medical student fill him in on the details of Henry's medical situation.

CHAPTER 35

Michael sat at his desk in the hospital, staring at the blank computer screen in the dark room. He failed. He hadn't saved Henry. He missed something, some clue or sign. He should have paid more attention to Henry's medical history, or to his lab results, or something. Henry should never have been allowed to leave the hospital yesterday. There must have been some clue that he missed. Something.

Every time he closed his eyes, he saw Henry looking at him, full of trust. He told Henry not to worry. Said he'd take care of him. Told him that he'd seen countless cases like Henry's and that Henry still had a lot of life left to live.

Henry believed in him. Henry died.

He should have been at the hospital sooner. Henry might have survived surgery if he scrubbed in ten minutes earlier. Five minutes earlier. He got there too late. The nurses all knew that. The anesthesiologist knew that. Even the medical student who scrubbed in to watch the surgery knew. Henry's death was Michael's fault.

He should resign. Or turn himself in to the medical board and give up his license to practice medicine. A good man like

Henry deserved to live a lot longer. Henry didn't deserve to die on the operation room table after three hours of surgery. Henry's family didn't deserve the pain caused by his death. His daughter's face crumpled when he sat down across from her in the private waiting room, the room reserved for telling families bad news. The room that had couches and boxes of tissues on every flat surface.

Henry's daughter thanked Michael through her tears. Thanked him for trying to save Henry. Hugged him. Told him that she knew her father's heart had failed him. Told him that she believed that her father was now in a better place. Told him that she was sad but knew that her father wouldn't feel pain anymore.

And it was his fault.

There used to be a time when he cried after losing a patient. Or got angry. Not anymore. He felt nothing. Like all his feelings died on the operating table.

A soft knock sounded on his office door. He looked over in time to see the door open and a hand reach through to the light switch. He blinked in response to the bright overhead light. A cleaner stepped through the open door. Not Ashley. Not anyone he recognized.

She took several steps into the room before she saw him. Her eyes widened and her jaw dropped open. "I'm so sorry. I didn't know you were in here. The lights were off and the door was closed." She glanced over her shoulder.

Michael stared. Her hair color matched Ashley's hair. Her scrubs were the same color as Ashley's. Her height was similar too. But she wasn't Ashley.

She took a step backward. "Are you ok? I can come back and clean later."

Ashley deserved better than him. She needed someone who could devote himself to a relationship. Someone who was fully human. Someone who wasn't dead inside.

"Your cell phone is ringing." She bent down to the floor and picked up his cell phone. He didn't remember leaving it there. She placed it on the desk in front of him and backed up again.

He should call Ashley. Call her and end things before he hurt her. Before she realized how much he loved her. Before she felt the same way. Before she found out that he was a fraud, a failure, and looked at him with every ounce of disgust that he deserved.

"Do you need anything? Water? Or maybe I can call someone for you?" The cleaner stared at him like he had two heads. Exactly the way Ashley would look at him if she learned the truth about how he failed.

He looked back at the computer screen. He'd need to write up a report on Henry's case. Get it to Dr. Evans for hospital review. Let everyone see his failure.

The door to his office clicked shut. Silence surrounded him. He broke out in a cold sweat, and the room started closing in. Michael bent forward and held his head in his hands. The familiar pain in his chest grew. Even if he could, it was too late to fight off the panic attack.

He let the darkness roll over him.

CHAPTER 36

Ashley stood in the office doorway, unsure about what to do. Her instinct had been right. He was lying on the couch in his office, eyes closed.

Something must have happened that afternoon. When she finished the cooking interview with Jeff, she couldn't contact Michael. She wanted him to be the first to hear her news. She called Jeff because she was desperate for a job, but now that she had an offer . . . she never imagined she would feel this way about a job offer. Especially a job as a cook, with a starting salary that was twice her salary at the hospital. He barely blinked when he found out about her lack of experience and formal training.

There was no way she would refuse the job offer. She'd had too much time to think over the past few days, more time for thinking than she'd had in years. Her parents were mad when they found out that she wanted to drop out of college and enroll in a culinary school. But that was years ago. Avoiding her true calling as a chef would never bring her parents back from the grave.

She needed to live her own life on her own terms. She

couldn't let the fear of disappointing other people control her actions anymore.

That meant finding Michael, telling him about the job, about her parents' last words with her, and removing the last walls she had built up around their relationship.

But now that she was standing in the doorway to his office, doubt crept into her mind. Why didn't he call her back? Was something wrong? Did something happen after he left Jeff's restaurant?

She tried not to worry when she couldn't get a hold of him. As she had promised, she took the bus to Henry's house with soup for him, along with some leftovers from the cooking interview at the restaurant. She knew that Henry would appreciate the food. She was a little worried about him. He lived alone and had spent the last week in the hospital. Checking in on him would relieve some of her worry about him, and she knew he'd enjoy a few good, home-cooked meals.

However, there was no answer at Henry's house, and no lights were on either. She called his phone, but it went to voicemail. She had to leave the meals in a bag on his front porch.

By the time she rode the bus back to her apartment, she couldn't shake off her worry about Michael. What was she supposed to do? She didn't actually know where he lived. She could have called Kelly and find out his address from her. She also had Bill's number from when they all hung out a few days ago. But calling either of them to track him down felt wrong. It felt too invasive of his personal space.

The only other thing left to do was to look for him at the hospital.

And now, gazing at him asleep in his office, she started to doubt herself. If he had wanted to see her, he would have called her. But now that she was here, she didn't want to walk away.

Her heart pounded in her chest as she gazed at his sleeping body. His body was too long for the couch, causing his legs to spill over the end of it. One arm lay hanging off the side. Normally a strong, powerful presence, he looked vulnerable in his sleep.

Cautiously, she walked over to him and sat down on a sliver of space at the edge of the couch cushion. She reached one hand over, running it gently in his hair. Her other hand reached for his shoulder to wake him slowly.

She watched as a deep groan escaped his lips and he moved slightly. Before she knew it, he reached out his hand and grabbed her wrist. His eyes opened, and she suddenly found herself the focus of his intense gaze.

"Ashley." The word came out as half a statement, half a question. There was an underlying sad tone to his voice.

"I just wanted to find you, make sure things were ok. You left in such a rush and didn't return my calls . . ." Ashley trailed off as she looked at his blank gaze. Doubt crept in, and for the first time, she wondered if she had imagined the connection between them.

He slowly sat up, and Ashley shifted slightly to give him space. He gently took one hand in his, and she gave a sigh of relief. The connection was still there.

"How did things go with Jeff after I left?"

"The interview went well. Jeff liked what I cooked, and he even offered me a job." Ashley couldn't keep the excitement out of her voice as she spoke and was relieved to see a smile spread over his face.

"That's great." His voice sounded encouraging, but the smile on his face didn't reach his eyes.

"And that's not all." Ashley's heart started pounding in excitement. "I checked my email when I got home, and I got accepted into a social work graduate school! Can you believe it?"

He remained still for a second, as if he hadn't quite heard her words. She saw him mutter beneath his breath before turning to her and wrapping his arms around her shoulders in an embrace.

"That's great news. Congratulations."

Ashley hesitated. He was saying the right words, but there was no emotion behind them. Something was wrong. Michael shifted his weight forward, then stood up and walked over to his desk, where he had a glass of water. She watched as he took a sip in silence.

Ashley wanted to ask him what had happened after he left the restaurant, but she wasn't sure what to say. After several awkward seconds, he returned to the couch and sat down on the opposite end. He leaned forward with his elbows on his knees and cradled his head in his hands.

"Michael, is something bothering you?"

He closed his eyes and ignored her question. "It's a big day for you. Grad school acceptance and a new job offer. What are you going to do?"

Ashley frowned. When she didn't answer immediately, he looked over at her with his usual, serious gaze.

"I think I'm going to turn down the graduate school. I really love cooking, and the only thing holding me back was . . . well . . ." She trailed off. Michael seemed distracted. "I think I'm going to become a chef."

He looked back at the ground. "Sounds good."

Ashley looked him over carefully. She couldn't see his face. She just told him something major, and he barely heard her. "What's wrong, Michael?"

He stood up and walked over to the window. She still couldn't see his face. She rose and walked towards him but stopped before she reached him.

"Look, Ashley, you are a great person, and I'm really happy about your new job. But I can't . . ." His voice broke.

She took a step closer to him. "Michael?"

He turned around. His eyes looked distant and red. "You deserve better. You should have someone who can be devoted to you. Someone who can make you their first priority." His voice was flat as he spoke.

Ashley felt sick. "What are you saying?"

"I can't be that person for you. My patients have to come first. I can't promise to be with you when you need me." He turned away from her again, looking out the dark window.

"I never asked you to make that promise."

He was silent for a few seconds. When he spoke again, his voice had a rough edge. "What kind of partner would I be if I can't be there for the important things? How will you feel when I'm late to come home because of a patient? Or when I'm called in to work on the weekend or miss your birthday for an emergency surgery? You deserve better."

Ashley took a small step back. What was happening? Everything had been so great this week. It was like she was standing in front of a different man, someone she'd never met, someone who was the exact opposite of the man she was falling for. "Michael, what happened after you left today?"

He let out a loud breath. "Henry died. I operated on him, and he died. If I had been more focused, I would have been home today instead of at the restaurant. I would have been closer, gotten to him sooner, and saved him. He died because I failed." He turned and started pacing.

A sob caught in her throat. "Henry died?" She had just seen him a few days earlier. He just went home from the hospital. She left all that food for him at his doorstep barely an hour ago. He couldn't be gone.

He didn't acknowledge her words. "My job is to keep people alive. I don't have time for anything else."

Her chest started to ache and her head was spinning. She needed to sit. "How could he die? I made food for him."

He stopped pacing and looked at her. "I wasn't able to be at the restaurant with you today like I promised, and I wasn't able to save Henry when he needed me. I failed both of you, and Henry was the one who paid the ultimate price. I can't be a doctor and be a boyfriend. I can only be one or the other."

She heard the words as though they were coming through a long tunnel, but they still managed to pierce her. She blinked hard. "You mean . . ." She couldn't finish the sentence.

"I have to take care of my patients."

"What about me?" She barely whispered the words.

"I want to be with you so badly. You have no idea how much I care about you. But we can't . . ." He finally looked into her eyes. "I'm sorry."

She took a deep breath. "Michael, you don't have to make any decisions tonight. You had a long day and need rest. Things will look different tomorrow." She looked at him again, pleading with her eyes. He just needed time to get over the shock of losing Henry.

He shook his head. "I can't. This is over."

She sat, frozen, as he walked out of his office.

CHAPTER 37

The next morning, Ashley sat across from Emily for Sunday morning brunch. The restaurant was buzzing with activity, the smell of fresh coffee and orange juice penetrating the air. Ashley ignored the noise around her, staring grimly at the untouched plate of pancakes in front of her. Her head throbbed.

"I can't believe this. I thought you two were perfect for each other." Emily sighed.

"I've never had the type of connection with someone like I had with him. Everything else in the world seemed to fade away. Just the thought of him made me happy. The way he treated me and talked to me was different from any other boyfriend in the past. I can't even explain it, and it doesn't really make sense. But I fell for him hard."

"Sounds like love at first sight." Emily let that statement hang in the air.

"Maybe." Ashley placed her fork down and looked at Emily. "It's like I'd never actually seen him, the real him, until these past few weeks. Maybe it was love at first sight, as soon as I saw the genuine version of him. Not the successful cardiologist version that everyone else sees."

"But he is a successful cardiologist. That version of him is part of who he is."

"That's why he broke up with me."

"Wait, what?" Emily's voice rose slightly and she started waving her fork as she spoke. "Don't tell me that, after everything he said, he dumped you just because he's a doctor? If he doesn't think you are good enough for him, then you're better off without him! Forget about him and move onto someone better. Someone who actually deserves someone as good as you."

Ashley smiled and shook her head. Emily was always so good at making her feel better and sticking up for her. "No, it's not that." She considered her words carefully. "He said he couldn't take care of patients and date at the same time. That I distract him or something."

"That makes no sense. Lots of doctors date or are married with kids." She stabbed her pancake with her fork.

"It does make sense, though, I guess. He was with me at the restaurant yesterday and had an emergency call from the hospital. He said that the patient died because he didn't get there in time."

"Are you talking about Henry?"

Ashley nodded and Emily continued. "I got the phone call about him last night. He was about to start hospice care, and I was assigned to oversee his case. I'm not surprised that he died. I'm sad about his death, but he was really sick. I met with him a few hours before he was discharged from the hospital. He told me that he lived a full life and wasn't afraid of dying."

Ashley considered Emily's words. Emily worked with many hospice patients, patients who were in the last few days or weeks of their lives, and helped the families navigate their deaths. Ashley didn't know how Emily continued to meet with dying patients day after day.

"Henry told me that he knew his time was near, but I don't think anyone knew it was so close. Anyway, I doubt there was anything Michael could have done to save him," Emily said.

Ashley sighed. "You should say that to him. He blames himself for Henry's death."

"Poor Michael. I feel so bad for him." Emily rubbed her eye.

"Me too." Ashley sighed and pushed around the food on her plate with her fork.

"Do you think we should do something for him? We could bake something together today?"

"He does like brownies. We could—wait, no!" Ashley crossed her arms and leaned back in her chair, glaring at Emily. "Whose side are you on? "

Ashley's eyes threatened to spill over with tears. She looked at her plate and stabbed a piece of her pancake.

"Sorry, I forgot about that."

Ashley ate a few bites without bothering to enjoy the taste. She needed to talk about something other than Michael. "I forgot to tell you my good news. Chef Jeff offered me the job at his restaurant." She glanced up at Emily as she spoke to catch her reaction. Emily did not disappoint her.

"Ashley! That's amazing!" Emily yelled loudly enough that the couple at the table next to theirs looked up briefly. "When do you start? I want all the details. Can you get me a reservation? I'll probably have to take out a loan to afford the food, but I have to go there now!"

Ashley held up her hand. "Don't get too excited. I didn't accept the job yet."

"Ash, you have to be joking. This is the perfect start for you to have your own restaurant someday."

"I know, but—"

Emily interrupted her. "Don't tell me that you are still worried about what your parents would think?"

"Em, they died that day. The last conversation we had was about how mad they were that I wanted to drop out of college and go to culinary school."

"That was years ago. Do you think they'd still be mad about that? Or do you think they'd want you to be happy?"

Ashley swallowed hard. She'd had the same conversation with herself for the past few nights. "It's not just that." She picked up her napkin and started ripping off tiny pieces. She couldn't look at Emily, not if she was going to say what was really on her mind. "What if I take the job and fail? What if I'm no good at it? I'm kind of scared to put myself out there like that." She mumbled the last few words.

"Welcome to the club." Ashley wasn't sure she heard those quiet words correctly. She glanced up to see Emily now staring at her hands, fidgeting slightly.

"What?" Ashley prompted her friend.

Emily took a deep breath and released it slowly. She held up her left hand, displaying the fake engagement ring. "I've been wearing this fake ring for the past three months. Almost four months, really. I was with Ethan for two years. Two years of him lying and cheating. I thought I loved him, but looking back, I think I was more in love with the idea of being in love. I didn't really love him. I just loved the thought of getting married, having kids, the whole package . . ." Her voice trailed off for a minute. Ashley waited as her friend thought in silence. "And here I am now, wearing this fake ring, lying to the world. Lying to any guy who might be interested . . . trying to make the world think that there is someone out there who might actually want to marry me." Emily looked down as she spoke.

"Em, you'll find someone. You don't need to rush it if you aren't ready to date again."

"Ethan is out there, moving forward with his life. I actually got an invitation to his wedding."

Ashley's jaw dropped open. "What? First, he's getting married? And second, why would he invite you?"

"About a year ago, while we were still together, he started dating my cousin."

"Which one?" Ashley was Emily's only cousin on that side of the family. Ashley tried to remember who Emily's other cousins were.

"Veronica. I think you met her at my parents' Christmas party over a year ago. That's when Ethan met her, too, and they started . . ." Emily didn't finish the sentence.

Ashley tried to remember who had been at the Christmas party. She didn't know most of the people there, other than a few of the relatives that she and Emily shared.

"They sent me an invitation to the wedding. Veronica even called me and asked me to go. We used to be close as kids. Which makes this whole situation unbearable."

"Are you going to go?" Ashley couldn't imagine going to the wedding of an ex.

Emily shrugged. "They're both living their lives, happy. Meanwhile, you and I are sitting here, practically sobbing over our eggs and coffee. You are too scared to become a chef. I'm too scared to take another chance on a guy."

"When you put it that way, we make a pretty miserable team." Ashley couldn't help but groan at the sad state of their situation. "At this rate, we'll both end up as old, miserable ladies who don't date. Sad, lonely, crying over brunch."

Emily and Ashley both stared at their half-eaten plates of food. A little kid at a nearby table dropped a plate on the ground, and Ashley watched as one of the parents leaned over and picked up the mess. At another table, an elderly couple conversed with each other. All around them, tables were filled with couples and families.

"I have an idea." Ashley leaned forward towards Emily. "We both stop being so scared and just jump."

"Jump?"

"Jump off the figurative cliff. Take a risk. If we fail, we fail together. I'll take the job with Chef Jeff. You take off the ring and start going on dates again. No more fear."

Emily grinned and slipped the ring off her finger. She raised her mug of coffee, and Ashley raised hers as well. They clinked mugs in the middle as Emily toasted. "Here's to making a new start, and no longer letting fear stand in the way."

"Cheers to that," Ashley responded. She took a sip of her coffee. "I better call Jeff and tell him I'll take the job. After that, want to go car shopping with me?"

"Sure."

"And maybe we can find a man for you?"

Emily coughed into her coffee and turned red. "Let's just focus on the car for now."

The server passed by the table, dropping off the bill, and Ashley reached for it first. "I'm paying today. My treat, to celebrate my new job."

Emily reached out and snatched the bill from her with a sly grin. "No! I'm treating you to breakfast. You can treat me to a meal at your restaurant after you get your first paycheck."

Ashley shrugged. The days of ordering the least expensive item on the menu were about to be over. She could actually start enjoying her life more instead of living in constant worry about making ends meet. All while cooking every day.

She opened her purse to pull out a few dollars to leave as the tip. If Emily was going to pay for the meal, she would leave a generous tip for the server. A small piece of paper fluttered to the ground as she pulled out her wallet. She automatically bent over and picked it up.

She recognized the paper as soon as she turned it over. The handwriting was sloppy and barely legible. But the numbers on it were crystal clear.

It was the note he'd left on her locker that embarrassing evening when she barged into his office while he was wearing nothing but a towel. He was as poised as an underwear model, and she practically ran away like someone who'd never even talked with a member of the opposite sex before. He left her the note the next day, but she didn't even read it until she was back in his office. That must have been the night she fell asleep at work from exhaustion, and he covered for her. Back then, she had no idea how kind and considerate he was or how persistent he could be. He never doubted their connection. He convinced her, each step along the way, that the difference in their jobs had no impact on their ability to be together. He showed her that he cared about her, not about her job title.

He believed in their relationship enough that he didn't give up when she put up one wall after another. He just kept breaking through.

She folded the small piece of paper and tucked it carefully into her wallet, between the remaining bills.

"Emily, I need to take that jump."

"Right." Emily didn't look up as she signed her name on the receipt. "Ready to call Chef Jeff?"

"No. I need a ride to Michael's house."

Emily looked up, eyes wide. "Does this mean . . . ?"

"Yes. I need to get him back."

CHAPTER 38

The morning hit Michael like a ton of bricks. Last night had been rough. He had to put together a case report on Henry's last hours, documenting the steps he'd taken throughout the surgery. It was standard protocol for when a patient died in the operating room, but each stroke of the keypad felt like a stab in his chest. Each paragraph was a story of how he had failed.

Dr. Evans was scheduled to review the case that morning, even though it was Sunday. That was one of the more stressful parts of working at this hospital for less than a year. All of his work was under extra scrutiny. If one of his patients died while under his care, the case needed review within twenty-four hours. He'd know by the end of the day whether he'd still have the respect and trust of his department or whether his license to practice medicine would be in jeopardy.

He reviewed the details of the case while he showered and got prepared for the morning. Each detail of the case was committed to memory, along with a clear explanation for each of his choices. He didn't regret any of his decisions during surgery. He only regretted that he wasn't at the hospital sooner.

And Ashley. He regretted that he started something with Ashley that he couldn't finish. He regretted hurting her when he had to end things. He tricked himself into believing that he could have it all. He would have to handle the pain he caused to himself. But he couldn't forgive himself for hurting Ashley.

By midmorning, he felt like a broken man as he walked to Dr. Evans's office. It was time to face the music. Time to sit across from the stern cardiologist and review Henry's case.

He knocked on the partially open door to Dr. Evans's office and entered cautiously. The older man motioned for him to close the door and sit as he finished a phone call. Michael obediently sat.

Moments later, Dr. Evans hung up and turned to Michael, his face unreadable. "I reviewed the case file this morning, and I have a few observations that I want to share with you."

Michael swallowed. "If I may, I'd like to explain a few things first. On Saturday—"

"No need to explain anything yet. The case summary was very thorough, and I believe I have a good understanding."

Michael frowned and shifted uncomfortably in his chair.

Dr. Evans continued. "First, I have to commend you on your work on this case. From the ER report, he was in very poor condition when he arrived. The fact that you were able to operate on him for several hours was astonishing. I have seen very few surgeons who could have operated with the level of skill that you demonstrated."

Michael's mouth dropped open.

"Second, I took the liberty of looking through the patient's file for the last year. I understand that you took over his case several months ago and operated on him soon after you started working at this hospital. Your management of his case was outstanding. Most surgeons would not have been able to perform that first surgery as well as you had. I believe that, had he been under the care of a less talented cardiologist, he would likely have died months ago. You did an outstanding job on this case and should be proud of your work."

Michael stared at him, momentarily speechless. "Th-thank you." He started to stand, but Dr. Evans motioned for him to remain seated.

"Now that we've covered the business side of things, I'd like to talk to you about a personal matter." Dr. Evans waited for Michael to respond.

Michael frowned. He was no longer facing blame for Henry's death, but was Dr. Evans still upset about that stupid magazine article? Or about the rumors regarding Ashley? He swallowed hard. "What type of personal matter?"

"I don't normally say this, but, you are a moron." Dr. Evans's face grew red as he spoke. "Don't look at me like that. I was in my office last night, and noise carries down the hospital corridors at night. I heard you break that poor woman's heart." A small fleck of spit flew out of the corner of Dr. Evans's mouth as he spoke.

"I-"

Dr. Evans held up his hand. "We are doctors, and we can't save everyone. But we help the people we can so they can go live their lives. You are a moron if you think you can't live your life too. No one is asking you to give up your personal life and commit every waking hour to the hospital. Have a relationship, live your own life, and stop being so worried that you aren't a good doctor."

Michael gritted his teeth. "I take my job seriously."

"You take it too seriously. If you keep staying late every night and work weekends, you are going to burn out and be useless for your patients." Dr. Evans stood and walked around the desk, sitting in the chair next to Michael. His voice softened. "Look, being a cardiologist will never be easy. You need to find your own boundaries and build your support system. You can't do this alone. You need someone like that woman—someone who will be there for you when you realize you can't save every patient."

Michael looked at his hands. "I don't know if she'll take me back."

"You won't know unless you try."

"If you think relationships are so important, why did you email me an HR document about workplace relationships last week?"

Dr. Evans groaned. "I didn't send that only to you. Hospital policy dictates that I send it to the entire department twice a year. I had no idea you were dating anyone until I heard you argue Saturday night. I guess I should have suspected something, though, when you weren't in your office each night last week."

Michael nodded sheepishly.

Dr. Evans stood up, signaling that their meeting was ending. As Michael rose, Dr. Evans reached out and handed him a business card.

"One last thing. Here's the contact information for a therapist on the fifth floor. All of her patients are doctors and other providers in this hospital. She'll be able to help you deal with your panic attacks."

Michael raised his eyebrows, his heart pounding in his chest. "How did you—?" Michael couldn't finish the sentence.

"She helped me with mine a few years ago. You aren't the first cardiologist to feel the pressure of this job."

Michael nodded and placed the card in his pocket. He had some things to think about. But before he could stand up to leave, his phone started buzzing. The ER. He answered the call as he walked out of Dr. Evans's office towards the elevator.

CHAPTER 39

Ashley pressed the doorbell to Michael's apartment again. The mechanical chimes rang softly through the door, just like they had done the last two times she rang the doorbell. And just like they had done an hour ago when she stopped by. No other sound came from the other side of the door.

She turned and made a thumbs down signal to Kelly and Emily, who both sat inside Emily's car. The wind blew her hair in front of her eyes, and she brushed it aside before scanning the parking lot again. A few cars filled the parking lot, but his wasn't there.

Hours had already passed since she decided to show up at his apartment and win him back. She tried to push aside the pressing feeling in her chest. The same feeling that made her sure that he was at the hospital the other day resurfaced. But for how long?

She scanned the parking lot one more time and then walked over to Emily's car and let herself in the backseat.

"Still no answer."

Kelly made a soft tsking sound while Emily turned the car on. "We could head to the hospital."

Ashley shook her head at Emily's suggestion. "I want to do this outside of the hospital."

Kelly pulled out her phone and tapped the screen a few times. "There's another used car dealership a few miles from here. Want to look at one more place?"

Ashley's heart sank at the thought of looking at another car. "I'm done looking at cars for today."

"I really liked the red convertible at the last dealership." Kelly sighed.

"Me too." Emily let out a similar sigh.

"Me three. But I hated the price tag." Ashley looked out the window as Emily pulled out onto the main road. A few cars passed them, but none of them looked like Michael's car.

"I guess I'll drive you both home. Ash, want to borrow my car tomorrow so you can look on your own while I'm at work?"

Ashley tried to hide the wave of sadness that washed over her. Everyone would be at work tomorrow, including Michael. She could practically see him sleeping at the hospital all week, returning home only to pick up clean clothing. He'd done it in the past, and she was sure he'd do it again.

She did not want to have this conversation at the hospital. Not where he said that he couldn't balance a relationship and his job. No, she needed to talk to him somewhere else, in a place where he didn't have all the reminders of his work. She needed to show him that they could get through hard times together. She needed to break through the walls that he'd built.

She saw a coffee shop across the street, and an idea formed in her head. "Emily, can you pull over?" This might make her a stalker, but she couldn't risk missing him today.

Emily put on the turn signal and pulled into the lot for a gas station. "You ok?" Both she and Kelly stared at her with looks of concern. Kelly's look was her typical motherly look of worry, while Emily's look was more cautious. "Are you going to be sick?"

Ashley shook her head. "I have to find him today. There's a coffee shop over there. I'm going to wait there until he comes home."

Kelly looked across the street to the coffee shop. "You can't see his apartment from there. How will you know when he's back?"

"I can walk there and check."

"And what if he doesn't get back for a few hours?" Kelly pressed her lips together and frowned. "I should just call him and tell him to come home."

"No." Ashley's voice came out harsher than she intended. "Sorry. I need to do this on my own."

Emily gave her a small nod, and Kelly didn't say anything further. Ashley got out of the car and crossed the street to the coffee shop.

～

Two hours and three cups of coffee later, there was still no sign of Michael. She glanced at the time again. Five more minutes. She'd make herself wait for five more minutes before she took the four-minute walk back to his apartment to ring his doorbell.

Three minutes passed by before a firetruck sped down the street in front of the coffee shop, sirens wailing. A minute later, another firetruck rushed down the street. Finally, one minute after that, Ashley picked up her purse and walked out the door.

Ashley turned the corner to Michael's apartment building and gasped at the scene. The two firetrucks that passed by earlier blocked the view of his building, and firefighters walked around in full protective gear. A crowd of people stood at the back of the parking lot, huddled into small groups and staring at the building.

A familiar Tesla sat in the parking space next to Michael's open front door. A firefighter walked through the doorway into his apartment.

Ashley started running. She ran between the firetrucks, ignoring the yells coming after her. She stopped right before she reached his front door when a large person stepped in front of her.

"Go back. You can't go in there." The man put his arms out, blocking her path.

She stared at the man, dressed in a police uniform. The high-pitched beeps of a smoke detector met her ears as she tried to push down the panic rising in her chest. She stepped back, then looked around. "Do you know where he is? The man who lives here?"

He shook his head. "Get back from the building."

She opened her mouth to ask again, but the officer's stern look made her words freeze in her throat. Two firefighters jogged past her and walked into Michael's apartment.

The police officer grabbed Ashley's arm and led her away from Michael's apartment, towards the end of the row of apartments. She glanced over her shoulder but didn't see Michael. "Do you know where he is?"

"You have to stay back. Let the firefighters do their job."

"I know, but I need to know where the man is who lives there."

"Look, the fire is probably put out by now. Give it a few more minutes, maybe half an hour, and your friend will show up if he was home at the time of the incident." The police officer's voice sounded nicer now that they were away from Michael's door.

"Do you know if anyone was hurt?" Ashley tried to keep the panic from taking over her voice.

"You can check with the ambulance." The officer released his grip on her arm. "Do not go back to your friend's apartment until the area is cleared. Understand?" He narrowed his eyes at her, all signs of any sympathy erased from his face.

Ashley nodded once, and the officer walked away. She looked around the parking lot. Michael was tall, but she didn't see him. She walked past a few groups of people and then noticed an ambulance parked behind the firetrucks. She weaved her way through the crowd until she reached the vehicle.

"Michael." The word came out as more of a gasp than a word, but the man sitting on the back bumper of the ambulance looked up at her. He started to stand, but the medic standing next to him placed a hand on his shoulder to stop him from moving.

"Ashley, what are you doing here?" Michael shifted his body sideways, pushing the medic's hand off his shoulder.

"Ma'am, you can't be back here. Patients only." The medic stood to block Ashley's view of Michael.

"It's fine, Pete. I know her. She can stay." Michael looked around the medic. "What are you doing here?"

Ashley looked at the ground. He looked fine, but she couldn't tell if he was glad to see her. "I came to, um, talk with you."

The medic turned his attention back to Michael. Ashley took a cautious step towards them. Michael patted the empty space on the ambulance bumper next to him as an invitation to sit. Ashley let out a breath she didn't realize she'd been holding and walked around the medic to join Michael.

The medic pointed to the ice pack that covered Michael's hand and his forearm. "How's it feel now?"

"Better than before."

"Keep this ice pack on it for a few more minutes." The medic grabbed a clipboard from the side of the ambulance and leaned against the side of the open door, about two feet away from Michael.

Ashley looked at Michael out of the corner of her eye. He smelled faintly of smoke, almost like burnt sugar but more intense. "What happened?"

"Nothing really." He looked at the ground by their feet.

The medic let out a snort. "I wouldn't call a fire 'nothing.'"

"Can we have some privacy, Pete?"

"Can't. Not while you're my patient. You should know that, doc." Pete didn't look the least bit concerned about annoying Michael.

"Pete." Michael's voice was heavy with warning.

"Doc. You two have your conversation. I won't listen in." He winked at Ashley. "Doc and I are sort of a team. We work together. I take care of the patients until they get to the hospital and let the doc take over. You can say anything you need to say in front of me. I've heard it all and I won't repeat a word." He looked back at his clipboard.

Ashley studied her hands. She did not want to have a win-him-back conversation in front of a stranger, even one who knew Michael. "Are you ok?"

"I'm fine. Don't even really need to be over here." He shifted next to her, his leg touching hers for a second.

"What's the ice pack for?"

"Nothing really."

Pete let out another snort. "I wouldn't call a possible second-degree burn 'nothing.'"

Ashley inhaled sharply. "You're burned?"

"Just a little. Thanks, Pete." He moved his left arm slightly, letting out a quiet hiss.

"Don't blame me. You started the fire yourself."

Ashley gasped again. "How did you start the fire?"

Pete put down his clipboard and looked over at them. "Hold up a second. The fire chief will want to hear this story. Ready to chat with him?"

Michael groaned. "Not really."

Pete shrugged and turned away. "I'll get him. Be back in a minute."

Ashley watched Pete walk away and then turned to face Michael. He still hadn't looked at her. She felt the anger start to rise now that she knew he wasn't severely hurt. "I guess he forgot that he just said he needed to keep an eye on you."

"Pete's a good guy." Michael raised his head and looked at Ashley. She couldn't read the expression in his eyes. "Look, before they get back, there's something I need to say."

Ashley swallowed hard. She needed to talk to him before he built the wall between them any higher. "I need to say something too. I —"

"This is Gail, the fire chief." Pete interrupted Ashley mid-sentence. A short woman in firefighter gear stood next to him, holding a notebook and a pen. "Chief, meet the doc."

"Nice to meet you." The chief held out her hand to shake Michael's. He shifted slightly so he could shake her hand while keeping his left arm still. "Call me Gail. Want to tell me what happened?"

"Umm . . ." Michael licked his lips and made eye contact with Ashley briefly. He looked back at Gail and Pete, who both looked poised to take notes.

"This is a legal matter. I need to know exactly what happened. We need to rule out possible arson."

"Arson?" Ashley's mouth went dry at the thought of someone having purposefully tried to hurt Michael. "Who would do that to you?"

Michael held up his hand and shook his head. "Not arson. Definitely not arson. I started the fire myself. On accident."

Gail looked skeptical. "Two neighbors reported an individual approaching your door multiple times today, about once an hour, with the last sighting about forty-five minutes before the fire started."

Ashley swallowed hard and looked at her feet as her face grew hot.

"I definitely set the fire myself." Michael's voice had a hint of hesitation. "I don't think anyone else could have done it."

"How did you start the fire?" Gail jotted down something in her notebook.

"I, well, I came home and started cooking."

"What were you making?" Gail didn't look up as she asked the question.

Michael mumbled something in response, but Ashley couldn't make out the words.

"What was that?" Gail stopped writing and stared at Michael.

"Mint chocolate chip cookies."

Ashley's heart started thumping out of control. She felt Michael's gaze on her but couldn't raise her head.

He shifted and placed his uninjured hand on top of Ashley's leg. "I was an idiot. I made the biggest mistake of my life. I wanted to do something to make up for it."

"I love mint chocolate chip cookies," Ashley whispered. She tried to turn her head to face Michael, but her entire body remained frozen, as if the wrong move would ruin this moment.

"I know." His voice came out in a whisper in her ear.

"Can you repeat that part? Didn't hear it." Gail's voice cut through and broke Ashley out of Michael's spell. Ashley looked up at Gail, who studied her notebook, and Pete, who stood with his arms crossed, an amused smirk on his face.

Michael cleared his throat and shifted his head away from Ashley's. "I said I made a big mistake, and I wanted to make cookies as an apology."

"What kind of mistake did you make?" Gail stopped writing and shifted her gaze between Ashley and Michael.

"Is that relevant to how the fire started?" Michael protested.

"I'll be the judge of that."

Michael let out a sigh. "I tried to run away from the best thing that ever happened to me. From the best person I've ever met."

"Did you apologize?" Gail looked less than amused.

"I'm trying to. The cookies were supposed to be a peace offering. But the oven caught fire."

"How?" Gail started making notes on her paper again.

"The oven started smoking, and then there were flames. I put most of the flames out with the fire extinguisher."

Ashley gasped at the image of flames taking over Michael's kitchen. She could have lost him today. If the fire had been any bigger, or if he had been trapped in the apartment—she shuddered and lifted her hand to wipe her eye.

Michael jumped up, ignoring the ice pack when it fell off his arm and made a soft thump on the ground. He kneeled in front of her and took both of her hands in his. His left arm had a patch of bright red skin where the fire burned him.

"You could have been hurt badly." Her voice shook as she spoke.

"I'm not." His voice was the opposite. Calm and comforting.

"We fought yesterday. And I almost lost you today." She freed her hand to wipe her eyes again. "Just like my parents."

"What do you mean?"

She took a deep breath in, trying not to let loose the sobs that threatened to spill out. She came here to make up with him, to win him back, and to convince him that they could count on each other. She wanted to rip down the remaining walls between them. But her body was aching to run away.

She took a deep breath and looked up. Behind Michael, she saw Gail and Pete turn slightly and point across the parking lot. They were trying to give her and Michael a few private moments. She squeezed her eyes shut, then opened them again and looked at Michael. "I went to college to be a social worker, just like my parents. Except that I hated it. I wanted to transfer to a culinary school instead. My parents were upset the night that I told them. They thought I was throwing away three and a half years of college and that I should graduate with the social work degree. We fought. They drove away that night, and—" she looked down at Michael's hands. "There was an accident. I never saw them again."

Michael drew in a deep breath. "That's why you didn't want to become a chef."

She nodded. "I didn't want to disappoint my parents." She swallowed hard and looked up. She could do this. She focused on his eyes and tried not to think of anything else. "I don't want to live in the past anymore. I don't want to stop myself from living my dreams. And I don't want to lose you. I love you."

He wrapped his arms around her and pressed his lips against hers. His lips tasted like smoke, but she didn't care. She told him that she loved him, and she had torn down the last of her own walls.

He pulled back from her kiss and rested his forehead against hers. "I love you too. I'm going to prove it to you. I have the name of a therapist, and I am going to get some help. Get my panic attacks under control again. And not let my fears ruin our relationship. I'm never going to push you away again."

Ashley moved her head forward and kissed him again. "Make me one more promise first."

He nodded. "Anything you want."

"Promise me that you'll sign up for remedial cooking classes."

"I will if you're the teacher." A slow grin spread across his face. "Maybe I can earn some extra credit by washing the dishes."

Ashley leaned forward for one more kiss. "I'll let you wash the dishes every night. My cleaning days are done."

EPILOGUE

ONE WEEK LATER

Emily took the beers from the bartender and glanced over her shoulder just in time to see Ashley and Michael kiss. She smiled and nudged Bill.

"They make a cute couple."

He looked to where she pointed. "I'd say so. Let's give them a few more minutes before we go back. Doesn't look like they miss us too much."

Emily picked up her beer and took a sip. She wasn't usually a fan of beer, but this one was good. It was light and had a taste of citrus. Not as good as red wine, but this restaurant wasn't known for its selection of wines. It was better known for cheap beer and greasy food.

Bill placed his beer on the counter next to hers. "So, what's your story?"

She looked at him. "What do you mean?"

He held up his left hand. "I thought you were engaged. How long have you two been together?"

Emily picked up her drink again, stalling for time. She left her fake engagement ring at home. Ever since that talk with Ashley, when they both decided to take more risks, she left the ring lying on top of her dresser.

She felt naked tonight without it. Vulnerable and exposed. But the lies came easily enough. She could tell just enough about her former ex-fiancé to make sure that Bill wasn't going to make a move on her.

But how would she face Ashley if she couldn't hold up to her end of their agreement? Further, how could she face herself in the mirror if she continued to lie?

Besides, Ashley had mentioned that she went on a few double dates with Bill and his girlfriend. If he was dating someone, he'd have no interest in her, and she'd have nothing to worry about.

"I'm not engaged. Long story, but I was engaged and now I'm not."

Bill was silent for a moment as he digested her words.

"His loss. You seem like a pretty nice person."

"I'll take that as a compliment."

"It was meant as a compliment."

Emily turned her attention back to the couple at the table. "Think we've given them enough time?"

He looked back as well. "I doubt it. We'd probably just be a third and fourth wheel at their table." He turned and placed his hand on the back of her barstool. "There's a place a few miles from here with better food. How about we head there and let those two have the evening to themselves?"

Emily started coughing and took another sip of beer. "I don't think so."

"It doesn't have to be a date. Just two single people getting together to eat after their mutual friends ditch them."

She narrowed her eyes at him. "Didn't Ashley tell me that you were just on a double date with her and Michael? I thought you were seeing someone. Renee?"

"Her name was Megan, and no, we aren't together. Turns

out she was only interested in dating me to make her ex jealous."

"You were ok with that?"

"No. That's why we aren't together now."

She traced her finger along a bead of condensation at the base of her glass. This could be a bad idea, but it could actually be fun—an easy chance to get back in the saddle again, so to speak. Going on a casual, no strings attached dinner with someone who was definitely handsome but not boyfriend material was a good way to get back in the dating scene. She hadn't been on a first date in over two years, not since her first date with that cheating liar.

She swallowed the rest of her beer. "Fine, let's get out of here." She turned to face him as she spoke.

She should have looked first. He was already half standing, half man-hugging Michael, who had shown up at the counter just a minute too soon.

Ashley was still seated at the table, motioning frantically for Emily to rejoin her. Emily sighed and grabbed her purse before walking back to the table.

It was probably better to avoid Bill, anyway. He was too hot for her own good, and Ashley described him as a playboy.

There was no reason to rush back into the dating scene. Bill belonged in the friend zone.

And that fake ring needed to go back on her finger before she made any more dating mistakes.

Curious about Bill and Emily? Find out more in Lacey's upcoming book *Don't Fall for the Fake Boyfriend*! Coming Soon!

To learn more about new releases and Lacey's goings on, sign up for her newsletter at http://www.laceybolt.com/doctor_signup.

Printed in Great Britain
by Amazon

72358537R00132